D0557694

A BRENDA FEIGEN PRODUCTION
A FILM BY LEWIS TEAGUE
Starring CHARLIE SHEEN   MICHAEL BIEHN
JOANNE WHALLEY-KILMER
"NAVY SEALS"
RICK ROSSOVICH   BILL PAXTON
Music by SYLVESTER LEVAY
Edited by DON ZIMMERMAN, A.C.E.
Director of Photography JOHN A. ALONZO, A.S.C.
Written by CHUCK PFARRER and GARY GOLDMAN
Produced by BRENDA FEIGEN and BERNARD WILLIAMS
Directed by LEWIS TEAGUE

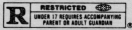

R RESTRICTED
UNDER 17 REQUIRES ACCOMPANYING
PARENT OR ADULT GUARDIAN ®

SPECTRAL RECORDING
DOLBY STEREO ®
IN SELECTED THEATRES

Prints by DeLuxe®

An **ORION**® PICTURES Release

NAVY SEALS

A novel by James B. Adair
Screenplay written by
Chuck Pfarrer and Gary Goldman

BERKLEY BOOKS, NEW YORK

NAVY SEALS

A Berkley Book / published by arrangement with
Creative Licensing Corporation

PRINTING HISTORY
Berkley edition / July 1990

ISBN:0-425-12455-X

A BERKLEY BOOK® TM 757,375
Berkley Books are published by The Berkley Publishing Group,
200 Madison Avenue, New York, New York 10016.
The name "Berkley" and the "B" logo
are trademarks belonging to Berkley Publishing Corporation.

1

The USS *Houston*, cruising at approximately fifty-five knots, made its way through the blue-green waters of the Gulf of Oman. Activity on board the large American warship was routine. It had been months since this area near the Strait of Hormuz had been considered "hot." All recent terrorist activity had been on land.

On board the *Houston*, Lieutenant Commander Claude Vetwether, the pilot of the Navy Sikorsky Sea King Air-Sea Rescue chopper, was lying in his bunk, scanning an issue of the *Dallas Times Herald*. It was over a week old but new to him; he'd just received it the day before. Vetwether had saved it to read with his morning coffee.

His copilot, Ensign Ken Trassell, was down in the communications room, trying to reach his family in the States again. In six days, Trassell would meet his wife and new baby in Rome for a two-week leave. They were flying in from Fort Smith, Arkansas, to meet him. During the initial planning stages for the trip, the travel agent had made a mistake in their connecting flight. Although Trassell was certain the correction had been made, he'd gone down to double-check and make sure everything was on schedule. This would be the first time he'd see his baby girl.

Vetwether reached over and refilled his cup from the polished aluminum canister. He eased the top back down on the coffee pot and placed it on his writing table. Smiling out from the silver picture frame on the desk were the faces of his three sons. The oldest was wearing a Naval Academy cadet's uniform with the rank of a junior. The other two in the picture were identical twins, about seventeen or eighteen years of age. Vetwether glanced at the photo; he hadn't seen his family in eighteen months.

Next to the picture was a small calendar with a large red circle drawn around the twenty-eighth. He would be home and retired by the time his copilot returned from leave. Years before, he'd promised his wife he'd get out after twenty years, and he intended to keep that promise.

Air-Sea Rescue missions were long hours of tedium and boredom for the pilots, occasionally interrupted with minutes of intense activity when the warning buzzer sounded and there was an actual emergency. Most of the time, though, it was a few hours of drill and practice followed by long hours of nothing to do.

The time weighed heavily on Vetwether; he was more than ready to leave. When he got home he intended to take his wife and twins up into the mountains of northern New Mexico for some high-country trout fishing. A cigar box full of trout flies

2

was lying on his writing table, a collection of bits of feather and line that were the stuff of fishermen's fantasies.

A rap on the door broke his reverie. "Ensign Trassell, sir. Request permission to enter."

"Permission granted."

The energetic young ensign burst into the room, flushed with excitement. "It's done! Marge was able to make the connection in London. She says the baby is fine and is ready to travel."

"That's great!" Vetwether said, enjoying the young ensign's excitement. "No more complications, huh?"

"Nope, everything is in order." Trassell was obviously pleased with the news. His freckled face was beaming.

"Well, now all you've gotta do is maintain your cool until you leave. Sit down, have a cup of coffee with me, and I'll share my newspaper." Vetwether liked this young man, who was only a few years older than his eldest son. They had more in common with each other than they did with any of the other people on the ship. The Navy's chopper pilots were a breed apart, the Air-Sea Rescue people even more so.

"You're sure I'm not disturbing you, sir?" Trassell looked over at the newspaper spread out on the bunk.

"Nope, I'm just doin' what I always do at home on Sunday morning, drinkin' coffee and readin' the newspaper. Here, settle in with the sports section. Read it and weep: The Longhorns beat the pants off your Razorbacks . . . thirty-three to seven!"

"I already knew that. . . . That's last weekend's

3

score." The ensign sat down in the chair at the writing table and poured himself a cup of coffee.

"Yeah, but I might ask you to read all the gory details to me out loud. I like to see my enemies crushed and humiliated in defeat!"

"That's pretty cold, sir." He picked up the paper and began to leaf absently through the pages. "It's gonna be great to see her. She was eight months pregnant when I left"—he made a gesture across his stomach—"out to there! Now she says she brought a STRING BIKINI to wear by the pool! Wonder what makes that woman think I'm gonna let her out of the room in that! And the baby . . . I'm gonna get to see my kid! This is just great!" Trassell ran a hand over his stubby red crewcut.

"Yep, it is that," said Vetwether with amusement. "In fact, if you don't let Marge out of the room, she'll be about eight months pregnant when you get home!"

Trassell blushed crimson red, causing his freckles to glow. "Well . . . I guess that wouldn't be too bad either."

A loud buzzer suddenly sounded throughout the ship. Vetwether and Trassell immediately hit the ground running, gathering up their gear, as they rushed down the corridor and out to their chopper. Everyone on the ship knew that this was no drill. Whatever was happening, this was the real thing.

In the radio room, the air crackled as a frightened voice sounded through the receiver: "This is tanker *Kuwaiti Star.* MAYDAY, MAYDAY! Over."

The radioman clicked up the switch and in a smooth, professional voice, said, "Shepherd here,

Kuwaiti Star, this is United States warship *Houston*. What is your situation? Over."

On the deck, accompanied by the high-pitched sound of whining turbines, the big Sikorsky chopper lifted off and began its climb high over the ship. Vetwether was behind the main controls, with Trassell beside him. The others, a medic and three crewmen, were busy sorting out their gear and preparing to load any casualties as the chopper streaked over the gulf. Vetwether monitored the radio connection with the stricken tanker.

"We have been attacked. We have five wounded, very bad. Please come now!" called the tanker's radioman, his voice crackling with fear.

Vetwether peered out through the Plexiglas bubble of the big chopper, his eyes scanning the vast expanse of water stretching out beyond him. Suddenly Trassell barked into the mike, "There, sir! At about two o'clock! I see the smoke."

"Right! I see it," responded Vetwether. He flipped the radio switch. "Shepherd . . . this is Nightingale. We've got visual contact one-three-five northwest. Repeat, one-three-five northwest. Searching for radio contact. ETA . . . three minutes. Over."

"Shepherd here. Nightingale, proceed posthaste . . . with caution. Over."

The plume of smoke was growing larger across the waters as the Sikorsky Sea King drew nearer the floundering tanker. Oil poured through the punctured hull and foamed out over the top of the water. Flames licked up into the sky and jumped from the tanker to the oil spill. The water arour 1 the *Kuwaiti Star* was a rippling, cresting, sea of 1 re.

Inside the Sikorsky, Vetwether looked over his

shoulder at the medic and the three sailors crouched by the door winch. He thumbed the intercom. "Get ready." Switching his mike to the warship radio operator, he called the *Houston*. "Shepherd, I have radio and visual surface contact with the tanker, bearing two-zero-niner. Range one-five. Vessel is on fire and adrift. Over."

"Uh, roger, Nightingale, this is Shepherd. Advise stand by till gunship reaches your sector. Over."

"Uh, negative, Shepherd, can't wait. They have five criticals and situation unstable. Request permission to go in. Over." Vetwether could see people on the deck of the tanker waving frantically at the chopper.

There was a long pause; then the voice of "Shepherd" sounded out again: "Roger, Nightingale, but watch yourself. Over."

"Roger that, Shepherd. Over." Vetwether then radioed the tanker: "*Kuwaiti Star*, stand by, we are coming in."

The tanker radioman sounded relieved as he replied, "Yes, thank you! Thank you . . ."

Banking hard to the left, Vetwether headed the chopper down to the weather side of the tanker. He turned to Trassell. "Okay, let's do what we get paid the big bucks for!"

Trassell smiled and nodded back to him as the crew prepared the winch to board the wounded. Suddenly the radio crackled back to life. It was the excited voice of the tanker radioman. "Look out, look out! Speedboat on my port beam!"

Trassell's eyes swiveled to the tanker's portside. "I see it, sir. . . . There, about two hundred yards to the leeward. It's a gunboat. . . . Can you see it? It's

6

pulling out from the cover of the smoke . . . there
. . . over there in the tanker's wake!"

"Got it!" Vetwether switched to the chopper's
loud speaker. "Unidentified gunboat, I am a United
States Air-Sea Rescue helicopter here to take off
wounded from the tanker. I am alone and unarmed.
What are your intentions? Over." The gunboat immediately made its intentions clear.

"Jee-zus!" exclaimed Trassell, as an RPG round
whizzed past the chopper canopy. The rocket-
propelled grenade was immediately followed by
tracers from the speedboat's .50-caliber machine
gun. "Christ! They're shooting at us, sir!"

The radio suddenly went haywire. Agitated shouts
from inside the chopper and broken radio traffic
jumbled together, filling the canopy with incoher-
ent noise.

Vetwether yelled into the mike, "Shepherd, Shepherd . . . we're taking fire! . . . Gunfire from an—"

Shepherd interrupted the transmission: "Nightingale, get out of there! Say again, get out of there!"

Flipping on the loud speaker, Vetwether called to
the gunboat again. "Gunship, cease fire, cease fire,
we are noncombatants—"

The chopper jerked hard and yanked violently to
the left, as several rounds exploded into its side behind Trassell's seat.

"We're hit! We're hit!" Vetwether called into the
mike, trying to remain upright as the chopper started
to slip to one side. "They got our hydraulics! . . ."

"Come in, Nightingale, this is Shepherd. . . .
Nightingale . . . what is your status?"

The chopper was losing altitude rapidly, the ocean

7

looming up closer and closer as the cockpit tilted precariously toward the water.

Another blast hit the chopper. Vetwether heard one of his seamen scream as the man flew forward into the cockpit. Vetwether yanked his head around to check the damage. A hole had been ripped into the chopper's skin near the tail section, and white smoke was billowing into the cabin. The seaman was lying a few feet away. He didn't have a face; the entire left side of his head was gone. In the thick smoke, Vetwether couldn't see any other members of the crew. Next to him, Trassell was coughing and choking.

"Come in, Nightingale! Nightingale, come in!" the voice rang in his headphones.

"Shepherd, this is Nightingale. I can't hold it! We're going down! Repeat, going down!"

"Nightingale, come in. Nightingale, this is Shepherd, come in! . . ."

The radio continued to call unanswered as the chopper autorotated, spinning rapidly downward. It finally hit the water, pitched forward, then flopped over on its side.

Coughing and trying to get out of his seat, Vetwether looked to his right for his copilot. "Ken, Ken, can you hear me!" He grabbed him by the shoulder and shook him. Trassell slowly began to respond. "Come on." Vetwether pulled on Trassell's flight-suit. "Let's get out of here."

Breaking through the cockpit hatch, they hit the water, still choking and gasping from the smoke. Their vests inflated immediately and they bobbed about for a minute, coughing and looking for the other crew members.

"Can you see anyone?" Trassell called out in the smoke to Vetwether.

"No . . . I think we're all that's left. Wait, there's Keaton," he said, as the medic bobbed up to the surface. "We need to get clear of the bird! It'll suck us down with it as it sinks. Get over—"

He never finished the sentence. Out of the smoke, a crude boat hook lashed into his vest, and two pairs of arms rudely yanked him up onto the gunboat.

2

Lieutenant (j.g.) Dale Hawkins faced the pool table. He stood with his back to the bar; resting his weight on his elbows. Hawkins was only half interested in the conversation taking place between the two men seated beside him. His dark green eyes were locked on a tall, leggy blonde across the room.

She was a coarse beauty, peroxided, heavily made-up and looking for action. Her battle dress consisted of tight white shorts and a red halter top that didn't keep any secrets. Amid catcalls and obscene cheers, she lewdly shifted her weight from one high heel to the other, taking her time as she selected a pool cue from the rack on the wall. Her hands glided knowingly over the cues, tapping the wood with her long red acrylic nails, but her eyes were fixed on Hawkins.

The bright neon beer signs on the wall made the three men in Navy dress whites stand out in the semidarkness of the room. They were conspicuous anyway, even in this small bar in Norfolk, Virginia, filled with dockhands and foreign sailors. There were a few other women in the bar, but of the group, the blonde in the white shorts was definitely the pick of the litter.

The girl made her selection, then picked up a cube of chalk. Slowly rotating the chalk square on the tip of the cue, she watched Hawkins. Some of the blue powder drifted down onto the tops of her abundant breasts, swelling up from the less-than-adequate halter. Without taking her eyes off Hawkins, she replaced the chalk square on the edge of the pool table. Smiling, she flicked at the chalk powder on her bosom with her free hand.

Hawkins and his two friends were each about six feet tall, with closely cropped hair, and all of them were what most women would describe as good-looking. Hawkins had an air of danger about him, with crazy-looking green eyes in a face that could change from devil-may-care to deadly.

"Come on, Sally!" a voice on the other side of the table called out. "Break the balls!"

She ran a long red fingernail down between her breasts and then blew on her fingertip, as if it were hot. Confident that she had the attention of the man leaning against the bar, she sensuously leaned forward across the table.

"Don't rush me. . . . I'm concentratin'." She winked at her target in the dress whites, then deftly popped the cue ball, sending the balls flying around the table.

Pleased with her shot, the woman straightened up and gyrated around the table to take her next one, her hips moving to the beat of Springsteen's "Born in the USA," which belted out of the jukebox at the

12

end of the room. The rowdy bar roared with cheers from the motley crowd of spectators. As she bent over to take her next shot, she flipped a look over her shoulder.

Hawkins hadn't missed a move. Next to Hawkins at the bar was Petty Office Billy Graham. Graham's fingers were tightly wrapped around a book, *The Rise and Fall of the Great Powers*. On his left was Lieutenant James Curran, who was trying to wrest the book from his hands.

"Clancy," Graham called out to the barkeep, pulling the book well away from Curran's passes. "Bring us another round!"

"No, dammit, Billy! We're late already!" Curran pounced on Graham's hands and tried to pull the book away.

The bartender looked at Graham, waited for a minute, then poured rye into the three waiting glasses. Curran sighed in desperation as the drinks appeared on the counter in front of them. Graham's hand flashed out and grabbed his glass, downing the rye in one gulp.

"Leave it alone, Curran," Hawkins said out of the corner of his mouth. He reached around blindly for his drink, fascinated by the undulating hips of the pool shooter. "I agree with you, Graham. We need another drink." He raised the glass to his lips as the girl shot another ball into a pocket.

Ignoring him, Curran pushed his drink aside and leaned over next to Graham. "What is it with you?" He put his hand on Graham's arm. "You've pulled five tours in the Mekong, gone balls to the wall with the wallies in Beirut, donated five pints in Grenada, stuck Mark-84s in Sandinista harbors—all without a blink! And now ... NOW, your spine turns to Jello?"

"You gonna drink that?" Graham answered, pointed to Curran's drink.

Curran shook his head and pushed it over to him. "No, drink it. Maybe you need all the liquid courage you can swallow."

Graham waited a minute, then nervously gulped down the shot.

Hawkins turned around to the bar. "And for good reason!" He patted Graham on the back. " 'Cause this is one of those through-the-roof, slam-dunk, grand-slam, top-of-the-charts, fatal mistakes!" He lowered his voice dramatically and stage whispered into Graham's ear. "NO one comes out alive!"

"Stow it, Dale," said Curran, pushing him back. Hawkins smiled and took a sip from his drink, glancing back at the pool game.

"You made a commitment," Curran continued to the confused petty officer, "and you've never backed down on a commitment."

Graham looked up at him steadily. He started to speak but then shook his head and raised his hand to signal the bartender. Before he could get his attention, Curran grabbed his arm and slammed it on the counter.

Hawkins put his hand on Graham's shoulder and leaned down to whisper once more. "There's still time to step down. Look, there are counselors for this sort of thing. . . ."

"Enough, Hawkins!" Curran yanked his hand from the man's shoulder. "Stay your ass out of this!"

Hawkins stood erect and straightened his tunic. "I can't," he said in mock sincerity. "I can't in good conscience stand by and watch a friend get sucked into the swirling eddies of despair and regret!" He was into cheap theatrics now, overemphasizing his point by making a huge swirling motion with his hands.

Slapping his arms to his sides, he snapped to rigid attention and, in a loud voice, proclaimed, "I'm not going to leave your side until I can talk you out of this insane idea!"

Curran and Graham turned to face Hawkins, staring at him. "You've lost your fucking mind," Curran said over the loud cheers that had broken out from the other side of the bar. The pool game was over.

Hawkins, still standing at attention, shifted his gaze up to the mirror on the bar wall. A slow smile broke across his face as a long, bare, female arm reached over to his shoulder.

"How about a game, Admiral?" the blonde cooed.

He immediately dropped his stance and, in a deep, somber voice, said, "Excuse me, gentlemen." Turning easily, he slipped his arm around the girl's waist and walked away, squeezing a cheek of the full white shorts. Graham laughed, watching Hawkins and the girl walk over to the pool table.

Its ring barely discernible over the loud din of the jukebox and yowling locals, the phone jangled at the end of the bar. Curran looked at his watch and stood up, picking up his hat and tucking it under his arm. "Come on, Graham." He reached over to the man. Graham shrugged the hand off his arm and watched as the bartender walked toward them, phone in hand.

"Time to ship out, Lieutenant," the barkeep said,

15

tapping the receiver on the bar surface in front of Graham.

Acting as if he hadn't heard the man, Graham picked up his book and continued his reading. Curran cut his eyes at him, then reached down and picked up the receiver.

"Curran here," he said into the phone. Then he winced, pulling the receiver away from his ear, as an angry female voice boomed loudly over the line. He held the receiver up to Graham's ear for a moment, got no reaction, and then interrupted the speaker. "Okay, okay, we're on our way." Not waiting for an answer, he hung up the phone and turned to Graham, who was feigning deep concentration on the open pages in front of him. Curran's hand slammed the book closed.

Graham looked at the book, then made a weak smile into the lieutenant's icy glare. "Time to go?" he asked, standing up from the bar stool. Curran tilted his head in the direction of the door. Graham nodded and threw some money on the bar. Linking an arm through Graham's, Curran grabbed Hawkins's hat and began leading his friend to the exit.

"Come on, Hawkins! It's show time," he quipped, as he and Graham passed the pool table.

"Shit!" Hawkins sighed, and he looked up reluctantly as the two men shoved past him.

The blonde put both hands on her hips and shoved her bottom lip out in a pout. "Do you *have* to go?" she whined.

" 'Fraid so, my darlin'," he responded, as he caught the hat Curran tossed. "I've got to go safeguard democracy and the American way of life. . . . But if I survive"—he stepped away, making a sweep-

16

ing bow in her direction—"I'm comin' back for you." He flipped a sloppy salute in her direction before sweeping through the door.

Hands on her hips, she watched him leave. As the door closed behind him, the blonde turned on her heels, smiled, and crooked her finger. A Greek sailor leaning against the wall happily moved up to the table to be next.

The shock of daylight momentarily stunned Hawkins as he emerged into the bright parking lot. "Zounds! Where are my shades?" He fumbled around inside his tunic, pulled out his sunglasses, and slapped them on, then looked across the parking lot for the car.

"It's indecent to do what you are contemplating in the daylight," he mumbled, walking over to the convertible. Curran and Graham were standing beside the car, waiting.

Hawkins suddenly stopped and looked at them. "Oh no! You don't think for a minute that I'm going be part of this funeral procession, do you? Not me! Here, you're so set on this, James, you drive." He threw the keys at Curran, who jumped up and caught them in midair.

Graham opened the car door, pulled the seat forward, and started to step in, but Hawkins jumped over the side and sat down in the back seat. "I'll ride here! You sit up front with Herr Commander!" Graham groaned, got into the front seat, and closed the door.

Curran nodded to Graham and slid in behind the wheel. The red GTO eased out into the traffic and made its way past the docks. An impressive array

17

of Navy vessels were in port, their gray shapes looming majestically out across the harbor.

Graham was quietly slumped down into the black upholstery of the flamboyant convertible. Hawkins leaned forward against the back of his seat. "If it's like every other time, Billy, you're gonna have a change of heart. But then, Bucko, it'll be too late!"

Curran looked at Hawkins in the rearview mirror as he slowed for the light on the Chesapeake Bridge. He came to a stop, then turned around. "And how long have you known Billy?"

"About a year," Hawkins answered.

"Yeah, well, he's been my closest friend for the last ten years, and I'm telling you . . . he's doing the right thing."

"For a SEAL, it's never the right thing." Hawkins snatched playfully at Graham's sunglasses as he spoke.

"Oh, GOOD! Now you're an expert on SEALs! How long have you been commissioned now? . . . Ten months, a year?" Curran caught Graham's eye as he had turned to swat at Hawkins and winked.

Ignoring the question, Hawkins slid back in the seat, then glanced over at the guardrails on the bridge. A glint of insanity crossed his face. "Billy," he said, quickly untying and slipping out of his shoes. "I'm not going to sit here and be a part of this!" Springing up, he stood on the back of the seat.

"Sit down, dammit, the light's about to change!" Curran pushed in the clutch, preparing to shift gears.

"Billy, if you insist on going through with this, I'm out of here!"

"Sit down," Curran repeated. "We're not im-

18

pressed!" The light changed and Curran hesitated, waiting for Hawkins to sit back down in the car.

"Okay, Graham!" Hawkins said, still standing. "It's the moment of truth! Are you going to do it? Are you going to make me jump?" He climbed up on the side of the car.

Graham turned around in the seat to stare at Hawkins, who was performing an exaggerated high-wire balancing act on top of the car door.

"Ignore him!" said Curran angrily, popping his jaw. "Get in the car, damn you, Hawk!"

"Well, well . . . Come on! Make up your mind!" Hawkins held his hands out to his sides, wobbling back and forth.

The driver of the yellow Cadillac behind the GTO began honking his horn.

Graham looked over at Curran, who was shaking his head. He turned around in the seat to face Hawkins. "Look, I don't want you to jump, but . . ." He took a deep breath. "It's too late now."

Hawkins cocked his head. "You're positive?" he asked in a low voice.

The horns were getting louder now, and angry shouts were coming from the cars lined up behind them.

Graham looked up at Hawkins; the expression on his face hadn't changed. Hawkins shrugged his shoulders, checked his position, then bounded off the top of the car. He glided over the bridge guard-rail and disappeared into the bay.

"Well, SHIT!" Curran stepped on the gas, and the GTO screeched forward, leaving tire tracks behind. Graham was still kneeling backward in the seat, a shocked expression on his face.

"Hey! We've got to go get him."

"That's a first! Pulling that stunt without a female in sight!"

"But he could be . . ." Graham's voice trailed off as he turned around in the seat.

"Don't worry. Hawkins is in his element. He's a SEAL!" Curran said, grinning as they cleared the bridge and pulled into the parking area by the chapel. "Now, come on around here," he said as he stepped out of the car. "Let's see if you'll pass inspection."

Organ music was warbling out of the little chapel onto the parking lot. Graham smoothed down his tunic, straightened his hat, and turned to Curran.

"I'm ready. Let's go," Graham said, with only the slightest tremor in his voice.

Curran grabbed him by the shoulders. "Stand tall, sailor. I'll be right by your side."

The side entrance to the altar was an old metal door that direly needed oiling. As Curran pulled it open, a loud creak echoed through the chapel. Inside, a large and obviously nervous wedding party audibly sighed as Curran guided Graham to the groom's position at the altar.

The minister raised an eyebrow in admonition to the two SEALs as they looked up at him, their faces devoid of expression. Graham flinched as the organist struck the first bars of the Wedding March.

At the back of the church, beginning to move forward, was Jolena, Graham's bride-to-be. Even under the white veil, thirty hard years showed on a once-beautiful face. She carried an enormous bouquet of white cala lilies and carnations as her brother accompanied her down the aisle. Both stared daggers at Billy and Curran.

Panicked, Graham whispered through clenched lips to Curran, "What am I doing? I hardly know this girl!"

"Good point," Curran whispered back with a sigh. "You've only been going out with her for three years."

"Still, this is a big step. Maybe I've been hasty," Graham said through the corner of his mouth.

"I am beginning to see that yellow stripe down your back!" Curran quietly nudged him in the side.

Three long blasts from the beeper in Curran's tunic sounded out over the Wedding March. The loud annoying tone sounded again.

Graham whirled around, his face suddenly filled with hope.

"Forget it," said Curran, as he pulled the beeper from his belt and focused on the digital readout. Graham peered anxiously over his shoulder.

"BAKER ONE . . . COME TO WORK . . . LOAD-OUT" was the message on the tiny readout.

"Damn!" Curran mumbled, then quickly looked up at the minister. "Oops. Sorry, Reverend."

"Then we have to go?" Graham's eyes were pleading with Curran.

Curran looked down at his watch, trying to make a decision. Not waiting for an answer, Graham stepped up to the minister. "It's an emergency. . . . We'll . . . we'll . . . have to reschedule."

He rushed up the aisle and intercepted Jolena. "I'm sorry, honey. We have to go. We have to load out." He tried to touch her face, but she jerked her head away.

"Now?" she said loudly.

"Shhhh . . . Yes, this minute." Graham looked around at the confused faces of the guests.

"This is some kind of joke, right? I don't believe any of it! Get your ass back up there!" she said, spitting the words out loudly through clenched teeth.

"I'm serious, honey." Graham tried to look sad, but he could tell that Jolena wasn't buying his act. Her face turned an angry red as she glared at him.

Pushing him aside, she yelled up to the front of the church, "Curran! Is he on the level?"

Pandemonium began breaking out in the pews as the guests turned to talk to each other. The organist, who had been valiantly trying to play on, struck a sour chord and stopped. Curran held up his hands to Jolena, nodded his head, and mouthed "Sorry."

Graham took advantage of the moment as Jolena looked up at Curran with hostile disbelief, and he hurriedly planted a kiss on her cheek. "I'll call you— I will—just as soon as we get back. . . . I promise." Wheeling around, he ran toward the door. He nearly knocked over a soaking-wet Hawkins, who was just coming in.

Puddling water on the floor around his stockinged feet, Hawkins struck a pose, legs apart and hands on his hips. "Hey!" he boomed out in a cheery voice as Graham hurtled past him to the door. "What's going on here? You finally come to your senses?"

Graham was nearing hyperventilation as he gasped out, "We got a load out!" He pushed the door open and disappeared.

"Load out?" Hawkins looked up at the altar to Curran, who nodded back to him. Hawkins started to laugh. Jolena walked over to him, swung back, and, with full force, pelted him in the face with the bouquet, sending pieces of lilies and greenery flying down the aisle. Hawkins only laughed harder and pulled his arms up to protect his face as she prepared to take another swing at him. Her brother grabbed her arm and tried to lead her to one of the pews. She was alternately sobbing and cursing Hawkins in a loud voice.

The minister stepped down from the altar next to Curran. "Maybe it was divine intervention, son. SEALs and marriage are not a good mix."

Curran stared at him for a moment, then tapped the prayerbook in the minister's hand. "Don't lose your place, Padre. That SEAL is coming back to see you." He then turned to the congregation and gave a hand signal. Five men in dress whites stood up in the crowd and rapidly left the church.

There were tiny pieces of greenery from Jolena's bouquet all over Hawkins's head and uniform. He stood well out of range at the back of the church, still laughing. As Curran approached him, he smiled broadly. "Time to go to work, boss?"

Curran glared at him as he walked by and out into the parking lot.

Hawkins turned to the crowd and cleared his throat. "Sorry, folks, but when you gotta go, you gotta go." He laughed loudly and swung out through the church door just as Jolena screamed and hurled the remnants of her bouquet through the air at him.

He raced across the parking lot and caught up with his friends at the car. "Damn, Graham, you almost got us all killed in there," he said, picking wispy green leaves from his tunic.

3

A brilliant full moon cast a wash of shimmering light across the maze of refinery pipes, giving the place the appearance of a bizarre modern-art park full of stark, alien sculptures. The bright moonlight lent a surreal appearance to the twists and turns of the structures and tanks. Things took on odd, unrealistic shapes, becoming studies in light and shadow.

In the distance, a dog howled at the moon while the distant horn of a tugboat sent its hollow, reverberating throb into the night air. The high-pitched sound of a *muezzim* leading his faithful in praises of Allah came from a minaret in the center of the little port town. The clanging of a buoy bell provided eerie musical accompaniment from the water.

A large black wharf rat, slightly smaller than a cocker spaniel, darted over the crates and boxes, stopping occasionally to stand on its back feet and sniff the air. With furtive movements, it worked its way through the stacked pallets over to the ship.

The rat wriggled its nose as it picked up an unfamiliar scent; then a series of splashes startled it, and it dashed back into the recesses of the stacked crates.

The only other source of light in the area emanated from the windows of a small, one-story office building near the loading area.

The darkness was abruptly sliced by the headlights of a shiny black Mercedes 450SL, speeding down the hill toward the dock. The top of the sleek convertible was off, revealing the silhouettes of two men inside. Screeching to a stop in front of the office building, the driver shut off the lights, but the two continued to sit in the car a moment longer. The passenger was chattering to the driver, obviously agitated. Their faces were obscured in the darkness. The driver was traditionally dressed in a burnoose with a turban. His passenger wore a Western suit.

As they got out of the car, the driver reached into the back and pulled a lightweight rifle from behind the front seat. He slipped the rifle's sling up over his arm and, showing deference to the passenger, motioned for him to go first into the building. As they approached the door, it sprang open. They were met by another man in camouflage fatigues and carrying an Uzi. The driver and the guard exchanged greetings in Arabic. The passenger ignored the civilities and spoke loudly to the man standing in the door. "Idiots! You shoot down an American helicopter, without authorization, and then you bring the survivors *here*!"

Holding the door open for the angry man and his driver, the guard made whimpering, apologetic noises. The man in the Western suit listened impatiently, then pushed past him into the building.

Off the main hallway inside was a large open room that had previously been used for storage. Several dark, bearded men in fatigues stood around the room, each of them cradling a German G3 automatic rifle. In the center of the storeroom, Claude Vetwether sat handcuffed and tied to a chair. The corpsman from the chopper sat on the floor between two of the Arab gunmen. The young medic, his eyes glazed, stared blankly at the floor in front of him. He appeared to have been injured in the crash, his face was pale and drained of blood.

Trassell, the copilot, was also bound and propped up on an empty oilcan by the door. A crude wooden plank table had been shoved in front of the pilot. A blank piece of paper and ballpoint pen lay on the dusty surface. Vetwether's chin rested on his chest as he slumped forward in the straight-backed wooden chair.

One of the terrorists stood behind him, smoking a cigarette. The man pulled off a last drag and threw the still-live butt at Vetwether. The hot ashes bounced off the back of Vetwether's bare neck, causing him to yank his head up and try to stand. The Arab loudly exhaled a cloud of smoke and coughed a laugh as the bound prisoner struggled in the chair. Several of the guards standing by the far wall had been watching, and they now joined in the laughter, chattering at each other in their harsh, guttural language.

The storage-room door swung open as the slender man in the well-cut gray suit entered, followed by the driver and the man who had greeted them at the door.

Holding a cup of steaming coffee in his well-manicured hands, the Western-garbed stranger walked leisurely over to the table. He impatiently snapped his fingers at the man in the burnoose. "Bring me a chair!"

A chair was quickly produced and placed at the table. The stranger was darkly handsome, with features so well defined that they could have been cast on a coin. He eased into the chair across from Vetwether and looked at the American. Motioning to one of the guards, he pointed to the bonds on Vetwether's hands. A guard stepped forward and freed the pilot's hands, laying the manacles on the table. The stranger slipped the cuffs and key into his pocket.

Vetwether pulled his hands up in front of him and massaged the red lines the cuffs had cut into his wrists. He glanced up from his hands into the dark face of the stranger opposite him. The Arab's mouth curved smoothly into a warm, friendly smile, but his eyes remained hard and dead.

"My friend Commander," the Arab began, "I apologize for this unfortunate accident. We misunderstood your intentions." He watched the pilot, then took a sip from the cup.

Vetwether stared at him, saying nothing.

"But," the stranger continued, "I trust my compatriots explained to you the need for your written statement?" The man flicked at an invisible speck of lint on his sleeve as he spoke.

Vetwether watched the man and rubbed his hands together in an effort to get blood flowing to his fingertips again. The stranger studied him over the top of his cup, pausing for a moment before speaking again. His voice was deep and controlled. His English, though stiff and formal, bore only the barest hint of an accent.

"This statement will solve all our problems. Come now, think of your own safety, the safety of your men . . ."

"No way," Vetwether muttered, looking into the dead eyes of the Arab.

Surprise flickered across the stranger's face, but he managed a laugh. "What is 'no way'? I am only asking you to acknowledge the truth: that you did, in fact, aggressively violate our host country's air space."

Vetwether shook his head and repeated, "No way, no fuckin' way!" Snatching up the paper from the table, he crumpled it into a ball. "Why don't you stick this up your favorite orifice!" He threw the paper into the stranger's face.

Without flinching, the stranger held up his hand and waved away the guard, who had moved forward to restrain Vetwether. The corners of his mouth curved down, giving his face a twisted, cruel look.

" 'No way,' you say? Oh, my deluded friend, there are many ways—all extremely messy and very painful. Just think, with a simple signature, you and your men could have been free. It truly makes me sad." He shifted his eyes down to the table's surface and then back up to Vetwether's face.

Sighing, the stranger wearily shrugged his shoulders, then nodded to the guards. "Kill them!" he said in Arabic. Then he stood up, pushing the chair back, and disappeared through the door.

The pilot's hands were still bound with a piece of silver duct tape. Vetwether glanced over at the corpsman on the floor and his copilot by the window. The medic was beyond comprehending the situation, but Trassell's eyes were wide with fear. Vetwether gave a wink of optimism to the obviously frightened man.

The man in the burnoose spoke rapidly to the guard standing next to him. Nodding, the guard walked over to the corpsman sitting on the floor and tapped him on the shoulder. The medic reacted to the movement and slowly looked up at the terrorist standing over him. The man smiled down at the young medic, then whipped a pistol from his belt and jammed the barrel into the dazed corpsman's ear. With shock and horror, the other two Americans watched as the terrorist pulled the trigger. The corpsman's head jerked sideways as he toppled over on the floor, a stream of blood and brain matter streaming out from the hole in his skull.

Putting the weapon back in his belt, the guard turned and pointed to Trassell. Two of the fatigues-clad men yanked the copilot off the oilcan and threw him forward into the center of the room. Trassell fell over on his stomach, then scrambled up on his knees.

"Get away from him, you bastards!" Vetwether yelled, trying to stand, but he fell forward, pulling the chair over on top of him.

One of the terrorists snatched Vetwether up from the floor and returned him to an upright position in the chair.

"Easy, sir, I—" Trassell started to speak, but the guard who'd shot the medic reached down and yanked his bound hands high up from his back. Trassell screamed in agony. The guard gave another brutal tug, bringing the copilot up from the floor. Trassell's screams seemed to fill the room, one blending in with the next, until there was no start and no finish. His arms were now above his shoulders as the guard yanked again. The joints in Trassell's shoulders stretched, creaked, then gave a loud audible "pop" as they gave way to the pressure. Trassell stopped screaming and passed out as the pain overwhelmed him. The guard laughed and threw the unconscious man forward on the floor.

The enormity of what was happening hit Vetwether. There was no escape, no way out. He knew Trassell wouldn't last much longer. Neither would he.

The copilot's agony was not going to come to the quick end the medic had encountered. Three of the terrorists slung their weapons and stepped over to assist the guard as the second phase of Trassell's torture began.

The men lifted the copilot's limp form up from the floor, one man on each leg and one on the ropes around his wrists. The fourth man took a deep breath, folded his arms over his chest, and began to jump up and down, warming up. A shout of encouragement came from one of the guards leaning against the wall in the back. It was obvious to Vetwether that the terrorists regarded what was about to happen as sport, some sadistic type of cruel entertainment.

The jumping guard continued to bounce up and down on the concrete floor, somewhat like a boxer dancing toward an opponent in the ring. With a powerful leap, he sprang forward in a wild frenzy, kicking Trassell over and over again in the chest, as he howled curses in Arabic.

"Oh, no! Please, PLEASE, NO!" Vetwether shouted as he watched the ensign's body being pounded by the impact of the relentless kicks. "No, God, stop!" He yelled hysterically, but his words had no affect on the camouflaged man inflicting punishment on the copilot.

The guards along the wall yelled out praise and support for the kicker, urging him on to greater efforts. Finally, the man began to tire and he stopped, gasping for breath. He made a motion for the others to drop Trassell. The copilot fell silently to the floor.

Several of the guards came up and clapped the kicker on the shoulder. He smiled and pulled the empty can over. Sitting down to face Vetwether, the man rested up for another session.

The copilot slowly rolled into a fetal position, his face toward Vetwether. A trickle of blood seeped from the corner of his mouth. It was pink, flecked with pieces of filmy tissue. Vetwether suspected Trassell's lungs had been punctured by an obviously crushed rib cage. The copilot's diaphragm heaved involuntarily.

"Oh, my God . . ." Vetwether threw his head back and stared at the ceiling. Hot tears of frustration ran down his cheeks as he evaluated their position. "Helpless," he thought, "we're going to die." The feeling made him sick. He dropped his head over on his shoulder, facing the window, and sighed deeply. Signing the confession wouldn't have saved them. These fanatics never just turned someone loose. They had already murdered the corpsman.

No, there was no doubt about it: He and Trassell were going to die. And he would be forced to watch them kill his young copilot first.

A fast-moving shape slipped by the window outside, followed by another, then another. Vetwether wearily turned his head to see if the guards had noticed. The guards, however, were turned away, watching Trassell, who lay motionless on the floor.

There was a series of loud clicks at the door. The guard who'd kicked Trassell sprang to his feet, knocking the can over in his rush. The door exploded open and a loud, quick, whirring sound like a pneumatic drill filled the room. The guard's body flew up against the wall, jerking spasmodically as each slug slammed into him.

A black-clad, hooded gunman burst into the room from the hall, still loosing rapid bursts from a silenced Heckler and Koch MP5 machine gun. Two men in the same guise hurled themselves into the room after him, both carrying blazing CZ75 automatic pistols. The attack was so sudden and intense that the terrorists guarding Vetwether were caught completely by surprise.

Vetwether, frozen in shock and unable to move, watched as the firing around the room continued. In less than three seconds, all nine of the terrorists were dropped, each caught in midreflex. The three men in black fanned about the room, firing make-sure rounds into each body. They spoke into the mouthpieces of Motorola headsets each was wearing. Realization began to set in as the pilot watched. The words that rang out in the room now were English—American English!

The first man called, "Clear!" echoed by the second, who said, "Clear!" The third gunman approached the last of the terrorists lying on the floor. He was about to make a shot when the wounded Arab lunged forward for his gun. In one fluid move, the third man laid him out with a swift, expertly placed Tae Kwon Do side kick. He stepped over the guard, fired a shot into his temple, then reported into the mike, "Real Clear!"

Hawkins's flushed face appeared as he yanked the knit mask off. He wadded up the hood and stuck it in his vest. Seawater dripped from his black fatigues, mixing with the blood on the concrete floor of the storeroom.

Curran barked into his mike, "Squad B, in!" He pulled off his hood. Two more men, hooded and in the same dark wet fatigues, came into the room, both carrying MP5s.

Vetwether finally found his voice: "Who, who are you?"

Curran moved over to him, laid his gun on the floor beside the pilot, and pulled a knife from the sheath wrapped to his leg. Sliding the sharp blade over the bindings, he freed Vetwether from the chair. "We're a SEAL team sent in here to get you out," he said, cutting the last of the tape that bound the man's hands. "Can you move on your own? We're going to have to haul ass out of here."

"Oh, God, yes! Just give me a minute! I can make it, but the kid's in deep trouble." He motioned to Trassell, lying motionless on the floor.

Leary, the team medic, closed the eyelids of the murdered corpsman, then swiveled around to work on the copilot. Popping a syrette of epinephrine, he jabbed it into Trassell's arm.

"Status?" asked Curran, coming over to his medic and the injured man.

"That guy is out of it now," said Leary, nodding toward the dead man against the wall, "and this one is hurt bad—correction, real bad! Massive internal damage. In short, these A-rab assholes just beat the balls off this guy."

Leary continued to work as he talked, trying to get a reaction from the injured man. "Hey, talk to me! Can you hear me? We've got you now. Talk to me! What's your name?"

Ramos, the team's dark, Florida-born Cuban point man, was snapping pictures of the dead Arabs with a small camera he had pulled from his sleeve. Graham rifled through the terrorists' pockets, removing papers and wallets.

Standing in the middle of the room, Hawkins surveyed the work. His eyes darted around the storeroom as the adrenaline pumped through his blood.

Finished with his pictures, Ramos walked over to Curran. "Okay, I got it, boss."

Curran handed the still-unsteady pilot over to Graham. "Help him out into the hall," he instructed him. Then he spoke into his headset: "X-Ray, this is Bad Karma. Extract in nine minutes."

Leary looked up from his patient to Curran. "We need to really ease him out of here. His system has just about taken all the jolts it can stand."

Hawkins moved over to look at the badly beaten man lying on the floor in front of Leary. Anger flashed across his face as the medic showed him the damage done to the man. "Why those lousy, ragheaded . . ." he began to mumble loudly.

35

"Secure this area, Hawk. We're heading out to the extraction site," Curran said. He helped Leary prepare the limp body of the copilot for loading on the litter.

". . . shit-eating . . ." Hawkins continued mumbling as he watched Leary loosen the litter tied to his pack and unfold it. The medic kept talking, trying for a response from the copilot, telling him that he was going home, reassuring him. Curran helped get the stretcher flat, and together they lifted Trassell onto it and secured him to the frame.

Out in the hall, Ramos had tried the door across from the storeroom. "Hey, I got a locked door here!" he called as Curran and Hawkins moved out into the hall, their weapons trained on the door.

"Blow it," Curran ordered the Cuban.

Ramos reached around and pulled a twelve-gauge riot gun from the scabbard on his back, fired two rounds into the lock, and kicked the door open. Seated on the floor in front of them was a dark-bearded man with no shirt or shoes, handcuffed to a radiator. He jingled the cuffs against the metal as the men burst into the room, showing that he was just a prisoner.

With his small camera, Ramos stepped forward and snapped several pictures of the man shackled to the radiator. The man tried to swing his head around as soon as he saw the camera, but Ramos had already gotten several quick facial shots.

". . . sons of bitches . . ." Hawkins was still mumbling his litany of adjectives.

"Looks like he's not here on vacation either. Could possibly be friendly. He's a rag." Ramos put the camera away and stood by the radiator, evaluating the man.

"Grease 'im!" Hawkins was teetering on the edge of control, the anger and excitement riding high within him.

"Whoa! Back out, Hawk. That's not your order to give!" barked Curran, nervously watching Hawkins. "Get a hold on yourself! Check the guy out, Ramos."

Hawkins glared back at Curran, the muscles in his face twitching with anger and tension.

Bending down over the manacled man, Ramos spoke in flowing, flawless Arabic. The stranger replied, speaking rapidly. Ramos straightened up and turned to Curran. "I dunno. He says he's an Egyptian sailor waiting for his ship to load up and head out. He says these guys thought he was a spy and locked him up. Sounds pretty lame . . ."

The stranger watched the men calmly, his demeanor giving nothing away.

"Egyptian sailor my ass!" Hawkins spat out the words.

"Hey! Hawkins, I'm warning you, get it together! This guy's no concern of ours. Just leave him where he is." Curran walked back over to where Leary was waiting. "Give us a hand here, Ramos."

As the three men lifted the copilot, the handcuffed man tried to disguise his amazement when he glimpsed the bodies of his men lying on the floor of the storeroom.

Hawkins watched as the man craned his neck to see more. "Check it out . . . *sailor* . . . that's how the United States of America kicks ass!" he said.

The Arab jerked around and looked up into Hawkins's face. For a split second something in his eyes flashed and his demeanor slipped. Before he could completely regain his composure, Hawkins yanked his CZ75 up, placing the cold black barrel of the automatic pistol between the stranger's dark eyes.

"This guy's a sailor, I'm the pope! Oughtta bust a cap in his ass right now!"

"HAWK!" Curran shouted. "Your job is covering our flank!" Curran was helping support Trassell, but his eyes were locked on those of his second-in-command. Hawkins slowly pulled the pistol away from the Arab's head. He glared at the man, then turned, reluctantly following the others down the hall. The Arab took a deep breath and closed his eyes, slumping against the radiator.

Outside, Alex Rexer, a huge, powerfully built man in black fatigues, had braced himself against a wall by the south gate. He was looking through starlight binoculars, which enabled him to see through the darkness and far out into the distance. Tilting his head, he spoke into the mouthpiece. "I've got traffic, six on foot, about one-five-oh meters south of my position."

The sound of Curran's voice came through the headset. "Roger, Ballpoint, put 'em in God's hands."

"Hello, God. Hello, God. Come in, son." Rexer adjusted the headset as he spoke.

A flat monotone responded on the headset. "God here."

Rexer looked through the binoculars to the top of the giant oil-storage tank towering over the shipyard below and saw God.

J. R. Dane, code name "God," was lying flat on the top of the tank, peering through a complex scope attached to a heavy-barreled sniper rifle. The rifle was a new one in the weapons inventory, the latest in precision firearms. It was an SSG sniper, a bolt-action with a silencer that covered half the barrel length. Dane, the team sniper, had added a starlight-thermal scope with an AN-GVS-5 laser mounted on the gun, making it as unconventional as the SEALs themselves.

Dane fanned the area slowly, scanning the yard through the starlight. Focusing on the area at the south gate, he could make out several figures running toward the extraction area.

Rexer's voice crackled into the headset. "God, I got yuppies at the south gate. They're moving up fast on my position."

Dane watched through the large complex scope. Six terrorists were clearly visible now, running toward the refinery. Flashes from their weapons could be seen as a U.S. Navy Sea Knight helicopter approached the area.

"I see 'em," Dane said into the mouthpiece. He switched down to the AN-GVS-5 and sent out a laser beam toward the approaching terrorists. The beam traveled to the target, bounced off, and provided the SEAL sniper with a digital readout. The microscreen flashed with changing numbers, then blipped a signal that meant there was more than one object. The screen stopped flashing, giving the exact range between Dane and the terrorists.

Graham, the senior NCO on the team, spoke softly into the mike: "They gotta die, son."

"So be it," Dane's flat, emotionless monotone answered.

Pulling back the bolt, Dane shoved a 7.62-millimeter cartridge into the breech. Slamming the bolt home, he took a deep breath and carefully took aim. "All ragheads gotta die," he murmured, then pulled the trigger, sending a round out across the darkness.

The lead terrorist was blown backward by the impact of Dane's bullet. Dane fired again, and a second terrorist dropped. A third man plunged over some crates, shooting wildly into the air.

Back in the office building, the handcuffed man sat motionless on the floor, listening to the action in the hall and outside. Feeling safe with all the diversions around him, he spit a key from his mouth, then scooted around until he was able to pick it up. In a well-rehearsed maneuver, he twisted his hands around until the handcuffs opened and dropped to the floor. Crawling across the hall, he yanked up an abandoned G3 lying next to one of his dead guards. With the rifle in his hands, he ran to the rear of the office building and slipped out the door into the yard. A pipe assemblage provided quick cover as a group of men rushed past him.

The chopper was approaching the pickup point. Ramos and Leary, carrying the copilot on the litter, moved out from the cover of some overturned crates. Vetwether threw the body of his corpsman over his shoulder and ran beside them as they moved out.

The Arab "sailor" leaned forward from his hiding place and took aim, fixing his sights on the back of Leary's head. Suddenly shots rang out from some scaffolds over to the right, causing the SEAL team to dive for cover.

Bullets sprayed around the waiting extraction party. "Looks like they've got a sniper, too," said

Ramos, as he tried to see beyond the darkness. He handed his end of the stretcher to Vetwether and stepped over to Hawkins.

"Yeah, the fucker must be on those catwalks over there," Hawkins muttered, pointing toward the scaffolds.

"God, this is Bad Karma. Sniper on the loose, southwest quadrant," radioed Curran, studying the buildings and pipe scaffolds for movement.

Dane swung his rifle around in the direction of the gunfire. "I'm lookin' through the starlight . . . nothing . . . switching to thermal."

He flipped the switch on the scope, and the image on the screen was transformed into a psychedelic vision of purples, yellows, and greens. He continued to pan until a bright red flash appeared on the screen. Dane immediately hit the switch back to starlight, and the flash he'd seen on the thermal scope was clearly identifiable. The Arab sniper was crouched behind a set of exterior stairs, his rifle resting on a riser.

"God says you die." Dane calmly pulled the trigger, dispatching the son of Allah to one of his seven heavens.

The stranger saw his sniper fall from the scaffolding and knew that none of the group in front of him had taken the shot. He lowered his weapon and pulled back into the shadowy cover.

A pickup truck with a mounted .50-caliber machine gun careened around the corner, its gun firing a long burst. Hawkins, Ramos, and Curran unleashed a curtain of gunfire at the truck, killing the driver and blowing out the front tire. The truck continued on up the street at high speed, finally crashing into the wall of the office building.

Several gunmen jumped from the back of the truck just as it hit the wall. Hawkins and Ramos began trading heavy fire with them as the chopper thundered overhead. Curran directed Leary and Vetwether toward a row of stacked wooden pallets, which would provide more cover. Graham moved up and opened fire with Hawkins and Ramos.

Curran dropped to the ground and crawled over to their area. "Hawk, you and Graham keep 'em busy. Ramos, you come with me and help with the stretcher. We're moving out to the LZ." With that, Ramos and Curran scooted across the ground back to the wounded copilot.

Snatching up the litter, Curran and Ramos raced across the road to the landing zone. Leary, Rexer, and Vetwether, his dead corpsman on his shoulders, followed.

Hawkins tapped Graham's shoulder and pointed to a massive pile of acetylene-gas tanks. Graham acknowledged with a nod and continued to fire at the gunmen, while Hawkins pulled out a tracer clip from his belt and jammed it into his rifle. He turned his rifle toward the tanks and took aim, unloading a steady stream of incendiary tracer bullets into the metal tanks. The loud twanging sound of the bullets hitting the canisters continued until they erupted into a blue-hot explosion with tremendous concussive force.

Using the explosion for cover, Graham and Hawkins scurried across the road, swapping volleys of gunfire with the terrorists. They ran into a large metal shed designed to protect cargo from the weather and ducked behind a tarp-covered pile of crates. One of the Arab gunmen's bullets flew past Hawkins, ripping the tarp and plinging harshly against one of the metal crates next to his head.

The stranger emerged from his hiding place near the office building and rushed toward his men, shouting in Arabic. "Stop shooting! STOP! Stop shooting!"

Hawkins and Graham heard the shouts, but they couldn't see the man calling out. A sudden stillness filled the yard as all gunfire ceased. Two of the Arabs split from the main group and disappeared into the darkness beside the shed.

"What the fuck now?" Hawkins said over his shoulder to Graham as they sat there, weapons poised.

"Who knows!" Graham responded, as the Sea Knight flew in low over them. The prop wash caused the tarp on the crates to fly around. Hawkins watched as the canvass flopped up and down on top of the crates marked "General Dynamics Corporation, Pomona, California." He squinted and rubbed his eyes to read the printing on the boxes. Leaping up, he lunged forward and gave the tarp a yank, exposing the crates.

Dane watched the chopper hover down to the LZ, then checked again through his scope. A truck was speeding toward the shipyard. Dane ran his tongue over his lips, focused on the target, and pulled the trigger. The round hit the front of the truck, causing the vehicle to explode and roll off the road, smashing into a concrete piling. A squad of armed men emerged from the back of the truck and continued running down the road.

Dane could hear Curran on the headset. "A and B rendezvous at the LZ. NOW!" He carefully slung the rifle up on his shoulder, grabbed a cable, and rappeled down the side of the tower. As soon as his feet touched the ground, he pulled the rifle around in front of him and made a dash for the landing zone.

Back in the shed, Hawkins slung his rifle over his shoulder. Kneeling beside one of the crates, he pulled out his knife and pried at the fastenings. The hinge jingled loose, and Hawkins pulled away the top. Inside was a long tube with a square box at one end. Beneath the tube were three cylinders in recessed wells in the packing crate. "JEEZUS CHRIST!" he exclaimed. "They're fuckin' missiles! STINGERS!"

Graham twisted around to where Hawkins was kneeling. They both stared into the metal crate with amazement at the most lethal antiaircraft weapon an infantryman can carry. One of the Arab gunmen, seeing that they were distracted, signaled to the man next to him, and they darted around a stack of wooden pallets.

Graham heard the sounds behind them and turned, firing as he did so. One of the Arabs dropped, spinning as he fell, his rifle pumping bullets into the other man. Hawkins was still kneeling, trying to unsling his rifle. "That was close. Thanks, buddy!" he said to Graham, a wild look on his face.

"Let's go!" Graham said, as, flushed and breathing heavily, he grabbed Hawkins by the shoulder and pushed him forward. "We've got a plane to catch."

The sailors on the Sea Knight helped pull Trassell's litter aboard. Curran, Rexer, and Ramos fired at the compound to discourage any terrorist heroics, while Leary and Vetwether handed up the body of the dead corpsman and climbed in.

"How's he doing?" Curran called to Leary, who was kneeling over the stretcher.

"Not very good at all, boss. I've barely got a pulse."

Curran hit his mike. "Extracting now. Everybody move it. Let's go!"

Dane ran up, swerving to miss a stack of pipes in front of him. "Hey Lieutenant, we got some thirty to forty hostiles coming this way on foot. They'll be here real quick!"

Curran motioned the others into the chopper and waited while Hawkins and Graham rushed up to him.

"Hey, you're not going to believe this, but Graham and I just found five crates of Stinger missiles!" Hawkins said, trying to catch his breath.

Curran stared at him in shock. "Couldn't be! You're mistaken."

"No," Graham answered, "I saw them, too! No mistake—five crates of the mothas!"

"We've got to blow them," Hawkins said, waiting for Curran to give the order.

"Hey!" Leary called from the chopper. "If we came to save these guys, we gotta get this one to the carrier or he's history." Bullets pinged against the side of the chopper as he spoke.

"That's the hostiles I said were coming." Dane crouched down and pulled his weapon up, looking through the sight. "They'll be all over us in sixty seconds."

"Hell, we can hold them off," Hawkins said, staring at Curran in the darkness. "Just give me some satchel charges and I'll blow those Stingers. Five minutes, max!"

Curran hesitated, then turned to Leary in the chopper. "If we extract in five minutes, we can be on the carrier in fifteen."

The medic glanced down at the copilot as the man coughed up some blood. Leary looked back out to Curran and shrugged his shoulders. "Your choice." Curran watched as the medic wiped the blood from the mouth of the man on the litter.

"Crap! We're out of here!" Curran waved the others into the chopper. He jumped in and sat down by the door, looking back at the building that housed the Stingers, as the helicopter lifted up into the night sky.

From the shadows, the stranger watched as the last of the SEALs boarded the chopper and the big Sea Knight pulled away from the shipyard. Hurrying over to the metal shed, he raced down the rows of stacked boxes, then came to an abrupt stop. There in front of him was an open crate, the top lying next to it on the ground.

The light from the moon danced over the Stinger missile, lying there nestled snugly in the packing material. The dark stranger couldn't quite believe the missiles were still there. "Allah be praised!" he said aloud.

He pulled up the missile from its cradle and screwed in a battery-coolant unit. Lifting the missile onto his shoulder, he flipped up the sight panel and pressed the activator lever. A second later, the warbling tone sounded in his ear as the missile's seeker locked onto the helicopter.

Long seconds passed as the stranger held the helicopter in his sight, his finger twitching on the trigger. Abruptly, he dropped the nose of the launcher and slid it off his shoulder. "No," he said aloud to himself, "we will not waste this missile. We will save it for something special." He stood watching the helicopter until it disappeared into the black sky.

The stranger then unscrewed the spent battery-coolant unit and tossed it off the pier into the water. Gently, like a father putting his newborn to bed, he replaced the launcher in its cradle and snapped the lid back onto the crate. Whistling softly to himself, he walked back to the riddled compound.

The SEAL team stood on the deck of the aircraft carrier USS *Coral Sea* and watched as the corpsman's body was pulled out of the chopper. Curran's eyes were locked on the motionless form in the bodybag. He looked back up to the Sea Knight as four sailors hustled out with the litter carrying the quiet, still body of the copilot.

Vetwether's voice startled him.

"Lieutenant, I . . . I want to thank you."

Curran turned around and looked at Vetwether. "There's nothing to thank us for, because we don't exist. You never saw us; this never happened. You got that?"

Exhausted and not fully comprehending Curran's words, Vetwether answered, "Huh . . . yeah, sure, Lieutenant."

"One more thing," said Hawkins as he put his hand on the pilot's shoulder, smiling.

"What?"

"You're welcome."

4

The airfield transport van pulled up to the curb and stopped in front of SEAL headquarters. Hopping out first, Billy Graham walked around to the side of the vehicle and lifted open the luggage hatch. He reached in and started pulling out gear. The rest of the team joined him, removing the gear and hauling it up to the steps of the building. As soon as they had removed all their equipment, Dane motioned to the driver to pull out.

An ensign with a trident insignia on his fatigues bounced down the steps to help Curran as he pulled his equipment bag up over his shoulder. "Good goin', sir. We taped *Nightline* for you."

"*Nightline?*" Hawkins glanced quizzically at the young officer as they climbed up the steps.

"Yep. It seems someone leaked that your activity was a SEAL operation. You'll hear all about it." The energetic ensign bounded up the steps two at a time and swung through the double doors.

Curran groaned. "No damn doubt we'll hear *all* about it. The pilot must have talked. Shit!"

Inside the building were several desks and glass cubicles. Large charts were stretched out over immense working tables, and several men, all in Naval uniforms, were working over them while taking calls at phones nearby. There was activity going on all around as the team members unpacked their gear and checked it in. Along the wall, a bank of televisions shimmered, their images flickering soundlessly.

Ramos stored his gear and walked over to one of the sets. He stood directly in front of the monitor and reached over to adjust the sound.

The announcer on the set boomed out across the room: "This is ABC News *Nightline.* Sitting in for vacationing Ted Koppel is Barry Serafin."

Barry Serafin's face appeared on the screen. Behind him was a graphic of a helicopter crash, underlined by bold text reading "GULF OF OMAN."

"Good evening," Serafin greeted his viewing audience. "Yesterday, the Pentagon has revealed, a shipyard controlled by Middle East terrorists was attacked by U.S. forces. The attack was in apparent retaliation for the downing of a U.S. rescue helicopter over the Gulf of Oman two days before."

"Ramos, turn it up! I can't hear," Dane yelled over to the SEAL in front of the TV.

The graphic changed, and the screen was filled with the trident insignia of the SEALs.

"Uh-oh! Listen up, guys: We're about to be famous," Ramos called over to the others. Stopping what they were doing, everyone looked up and joined Ramos in front of the set.

Serafin's voice continued: "Though officials won't comment, sources close to the operation indicate that the raid was the work of the U.S. Navy SEALs, the nation's top-secret combat unit."

"You're right, boss—our grateful pilot talked." Hawkins laid a hand on Curran's arm and watched as Serafin turned to another camera.

"On tonight's 'Focus,' we'll be joined by Senator John Warner, a former secretary of the Navy, and by prize-winning journalist and leading expert on Middle East terrorism, Claire Verens." The two guests, Senator Warner and Ms. Verens, were shown sitting at a large oval table. "But first, ABC News correspondent Peter Walker has a special report."

A video newsreel with images of SEALs in training appeared over the narration by Walker. "Their name is an acronym for *sea*, *air*, and *land*. They are considered by many to be the toughest, most elite commando unit on earth. But in a world where the United States is increasingly vulnerable to hostage-taking and airline-hijacking, where there are currently thirty-six guerrilla wars in progress, special operations units like the SEALs are increasingly seen as a vital compromise between failed diplomacy and massive military force. . . ."

A hand reached over and switched the set off. "What's really sad is that you boys are probably getting off on listening to this bullshit." Captain Dunne, the commander of the East Coast SEAL teams, stood in front of the TV. Dunne was a man in his early fifties, tough and ramrod straight. He stood with his feet apart, hands clasped casually behind him. "By the way, we got a report on that copilot. It looks like he's going to make it. Good work, Leary."

"Too bad we didn't make it in time for the medic," Leary said.

"Captain, we need to talk." Curran started toward Dunne, who motioned to a spot over to the side.

"What's on your mind?" Dunne asked, as they pulled out of earshot of the other men.

"Intelligence, sir. It wasn't worth a shit. You read the report: 'Maximum of ten hostiles at extraction site.' Sure as hell fooled me!"

"Look, Curran, I've been raising holy hell up there all day. Needless to say, everybody's passing the buck."

"I can imagine. This isn't the first time we've been fucked up by bad intelligence."

"Well, you'll have your chance to tell the story tomorrow. Dress blues and tennis shoes, 0900, Pentagon. Do yourself a favor: Blow off some of your steam tonight." Dunne slapped Curran on the shoulder and headed off down the hall.

"Come on, boss! Drinks are on me." Graham walked over and grabbed Curran by the arm, shoving him toward the door.

"I think you need to see someone first . . . don't you?"

Graham groaned and nodded to Curran. "You know Jolena: She's probably had all the locks changed on me."

"I'll give her a call; she'll let you back in."

Graham looked relieved. "Thanks."

"One condition: . . . You have a new wedding date on my desk by 0700 tomorrow."

Making a weak, halfhearted salute, Graham said, "Aye-aye, sir."

They walked together down the hall and stopped at a pay phone. Curran reached down into his pocket, pulled out a quarter, and popped it into the slot.

"Six-two-one, oh-seven, four-four." Graham gave the number to Curran.

The phone rang twice, and a voice on the other end answered rather crisply.

"Hi there, Jolena, this is James. I have your wanderin' boy here, and he wants to come home."

The voice on the other end rattled along for a while, and Curran laughed. "You don't mean that! It would ruin your sex life!"

Graham looked worried, and he jokingly covered his crotch with both hands.

"Okay, I'll send him along then, but you be gentle with him. . . . All right. . . . Well, he'll talk to you about that when he get's there. . . . Yes, he does want to marry you. . . . You know that! . . . Bye, Jolena. See you later."

Curran put the phone back on the hook and turned to Graham. "All clear. Now get over there—she's feeling weak."

"See you later, boss," Graham called over his shoulder, running down the hall to the exit door.

Curran smiled as he watched Graham leave, then reached into his pocket and pulled out his car keys. Jingling the keys nervously in his hand, he headed out the door to his car.

Dale Hawkins came up behind him. "Hold up a minute, boss." He quickened his step and came up alongside. "Think you'll get reamed for the Stingers tomorrow?"

"Does the pope wear a funny hat?" asked Curran sarcastically, as he continued to his car.

"Needless to say, I'd have called it differently." Hawkins smiled defiantly.

"Well, Hawk, it wasn't your call at all."

"One day it will be," said Hawkins flatly.

"If you ever grow up."

"What do you mean, 'grow up'?" Hawkins said, anger rising in his voice.

Curran stopped by the jeep and leaned on the roll bar. "I mean like 'That's how the United States of America kicks ass!' "

"Hey, James, I was overcome with patriotism! That's no crime," Hawkins avowed, still affronted.

"You know, Hawkins," Curran said as he opened the door, "as far as your skills and your balls, you're as good as I've ever seen. But you're just too damn much of a hot dog!"

Hawkins pushed Curran's door closed. "Explain that!"

Curran's facial expression became somber; the intensity he felt about what he was saying was obvious. "You have to learn some restraint. . . . Or someone's gonna get killed, and that someone might not even be you!"

Hawkins looked at him for a long time, not saying anything. He realized that Curran wasn't kidding and that this wasn't the time or the place to pursue the matter.

They stood there in the parking lot for what seemed like a long time, staring at each other, before Hawkins finally broke the silence.

"Are you done with the lecture?"

Curran nodded.

"Good . . . good, 'cause I need to take care of some business in Washington tomorrow. Think I can hitch a ride?"

Curran laughed and jumped into the jeep. "And what's her name, Hawk?"

Hawkins feigned innocence. "I don't know what you're talking about!"

As the jeep roared to life, Curran pressed down on the clutch and shifted into reverse, rolling away from him. "Wait, wait, Curran!" Hawkins leaned over into the vehicle. "Come to think of it, she does have a beautiful roommate."

Curran continued to back out of the space. "Well, Hawk, I'm sure we can work out something. Be at the airfield early." He gave a quick wave, then darted out of the parking lot and down the street.

Admiral Colker paced to the end of his desk, stopped, turned, and paced back to the other end, never taking his eyes off Lieutenant Curran. Curran and Captain Dunne were standing at attention in front of the admiral's desk in his Pentagon office.

"At ease, gentlemen. Have a seat." The admiral had stopped pacing and now stood behind a huge leather desk chair, his hands resting on the chair back. Dunne and Curran sat down in the two chairs provided for them in front of the desk.

"Lieutenant Curran,"—the admiral turned his back to the two men and walked over to look out a large bay window as he spoke—"why didn't you destroy the Stingers?"

"Sir, the mission was to rescue American personnel—"

"As a SEAL team commander," the admiral interrupted, "you are expected to adapt your tactics as the situation dictates." He still had his back to them, his hands crossed behind him, staring out the window.

"Sir," said Curran, "the situation dictated that I make a decision between destroying those missiles and saving a human life. I chose the latter."

"Do you know how many innocent lives could be put in jeopardy by those missiles?" Admiral Colker asked.

Curran waited a moment before responding. "I stand by my decision, sir."

The admiral turned around and placed his hands on his desk, leaning forward toward the lieutenant. "And so do I. Unfortunately, we will have to deal with the consequences of that decision." He stared at Curran, who looked back unflinchingly. "Well, we'd best go now," the admiral said. "The Naval Intelligence Committee is waiting, and we don't want to agitate them any more than they already are."

Leaving the admiral's office, the three men headed down one of the long corridors of the Pentagon's Navy wing until they reached a large conference room. As they opened the door, the conversation in the room stopped.

Curran felt ill at ease as he looked down the table of officers, congressmen, and senators. He found his place and quickly sat down. The only person standing was the president's man on the National Security Council, Warren Stinson.

Stinson was a politician of the first order, a polished professional who had worked with the president for over fifteen years. Rumors around Washington—a town that ran on rumor—had it that he was the president's most trusted confidant. It was no rumor that he wielded a tremendous amount of power.

He stood slouching at the front of the room, his hands in his pockets. As he watched Curran sit down, he reached up and smoothed his closely clipped mustache. When Curran was seated, Stinson slammed his hand down on the table in front of him and said angrily, "Why didn't we know the Stingers were there!"

Jim Elmore, the State Department representative, wearily responded, "The trouble is, we have satellites that can photograph license plates from three hundred miles away, but nobody inside, nobody right there on the ground." Elmore looked rumpled and tired. He was a senior man in the State Department who threatened to retire every year.

Nervously clearing his throat, Eliot West, the youngest man in the room besides Curran, started to speak: "Because of budget limitations, the CIA has had to cut back—"

"If you spent less time and energy working on your own agendas over there," Elmore interrupted the CIA man, "and more time on—"

"Hey," Stinson cut in, "knock if off. We're here for a briefing. Jim, you first."

Elmore took a deep breath and leaned back in his chair. "Here's what we at State think is going on. The Stingers we gave to the Afghan rebels are now finding their way into the Persian Gulf black market. This was our fear . . . and, need I remind you, our prediction." He shot a look at Stinson.

"Oh, come on, that's old business, Elmore, old

business." Stinson looked tired, and his voice sounded pained.

Elmore started to say something in retort but instead moved on. "The SEAL team's sighting is our first verification." He held up the photograph Ramos had taken of the Arabic stranger, then passed it down the table. "This is the picture taken by your team at target, Lieutenant Curran. Do you recognize this man?"

"Yes, sir, he was posing as a friendly. We later learned he took part in the torture of the American captives."

West laughed out loud. "In the larger realm of things, that's the smallest of his sins, Lieutenant. You need to take a look at your chance encounter." The CIA man reached down and hit a remote-control switch. A large television screen on the right side of the room blinked on. There was a tape in progress, but West zipped it ahead until it stopped on the face of an attractive brunette with dark, almond-shaped eyes. She appeared to be in her early thirties, tailored and fresh looking in a red camp shirt and a pair of khaki slacks. Her hair was cut in a long pageboy style and was molded neatly against her straight, clean features. The woman, Claire Verens, was seated at a table, leaning forward and speaking into a handheld mike.

". . . Kidnapings and hijackings are not acts of terrorism?" She extended the mike to the person she was interviewing, just out of camera range. The camera shifted and focused on the man. Curran flinched as the image of the stranger, looking distinguished and suave, began to answer the question.

"If defending ourselves against American, Israeli,

and French oppression constitutes terrorism, then, in that context, we are terrorists." The stranger had a pleasant, trust-me smile on his face.

Claire Verens spoke again: "Does that include the bombing of the Marine barracks in Beirut?" Curran sat up, his muscles tensing, and leaned forward, waiting to see what the Arab would say.

The dark, handsome stranger looked down at his well-buffed nails for a minute before answering, again with a slightly bemused look on his face. "If America kills my people, then my people must kill Americans. This path is the path of blood, the path of martyrdom."

"Are you prepared to be a martyr yourself," Claire asked the man. "Or do you prefer just giving the orders?"

Smiling, the stranger opened his hands, palms up, as he explained, "Death is our most sacred gift if it comes while fighting for the cause of God and while defending the oppressed."

West stopped the tape and turned off the television monitor. Curran dropped his head in his hands and took a deep breath, then looked up as the CIA representative began to speak. "A real nice guy, huh? All we know about him is his name . . . Ben Shaheed . . . and that he's taken over the most radical terrorist organization in the Middle East, the Al Shuhada." West reached down and took a sip from his glass of water before continuing. Curran watched him, feeling sick.

"We," he continued, placing the glass back on the table, "are fairly convinced that he was at the target to take those missiles home with him."

"A worst-case scenario," muttered Stinson.

Jim Elmore shook his head. "Stingers are the perfect terrorist weapon. Portable, handheld, lightweight . . ."

Stinson swung around to face Curran. "Why the hell didn't you destroy those missiles when you found them!"

Admiral Colker was on his feet at once. "Warren, it may surprise you"—the admiral's voice was strong and firm—"but we put a high premium on saving the lives of our men. The lieutenant made a decision under fire and it was a damn good one."

Stinson was staring at the admiral as he spoke, but he finally broke and looked away.

Colker cleared his voice. He spoke slowly and deliberately. "Gentlemen, the point is not what *should* have been done but what *can* be done now."

The quiet, forceful voice of Air Force General Mateen cut through the thoughtful silence left by Colker's last remark. "The Air Force could take care of those Stingers with a surgical air strike. In and out, quick and clean."

"Nope! Sorry, General," said Elmore, "but there's no such thing as a 'surgical' air strike. There's no way to avoid killing innocent civilians. I believe we know where world opinion would fall on that one."

There was a long silence. Curran looked first to the admiral, then up at Stinson. "If I may, sir." Stinson nodded his permission.

"I suggest you send our team back to target. We have firsthand knowledge of the site and the personnel." Curran paused. "With the proper intelligence . . . and preparation, I guarantee we'll take out those Stingers."

Stinson tapped his fingers impatiently on the table, then looked over to the admiral. "Colker, this is the president's call. We'll see if he wants to take another chance with your SEALs on this. I'll let you know."

The admiral nodded, and Stinson turned to Curran and Dunne.

"If we give you another chance, and you tough guys don't take those missiles out this time, we may have to call in Delta Force."

Curran and Dunne answered simultaneously. "Yes, sir."

Stinson looked around the room. "Well, gentlemen," he said, closing the folder on the table in front of him, "that's it. Let's go back to work. Admiral Colker, I'll get back to you with a decision as soon as I can."

Curran and Hawkins stood in front of the ticket counter at Dulles Airport, waiting for their tickets. Hawkins suddenly slammed his fist down on the counter, startling the lady behind them. "I knew it, Curran! I knew that fucker wasn't an Egyptian sailor! I should have—"

"Hey, Hawk, under the circumstances, you did the right thing. We didn't have time for proper interrogation and"—he turned and locked eyes with Hawkins—"we don't assassinate on gut instinct."

Hawkins looked up at the ceiling in desperation. "Yeah, but gut instinct was right! We shoulda wasted him!"

"You're such a cool professional!" Curran was preparing to dress Hawkins down when suddenly he caught a glimpse of something in the distance. "I'll be right back."

He leaped over the low enclosure near the luggage carriers and charged down the ramp after a woman walking toward a boarding gate. He finally caught up with her, nearly out of breath. "Miss! Oh, miss, can you hold it a minute?"

Claire Verens turned to face him. She was more attractive in person that she was on the TV screen. She wore a jade-green pants suit, and the color suited her, Curran thought to himself. She continued walking, looking at him curiously. "Yes?"

Curran walked along beside her, matching her stride for stride. He awkwardly stuck out his hand. "Hi, uh, my name is James Curran. I'd like a few words with you."

She smiled, but she didn't slow down. "Can you walk and talk at the same time, Mr. Curran?"

"I think I can manage." Curran pulled in his hand and noticed that she was carrying a briefcase in one hand and a camcorder in the other. "Oh, hey, I'm sorry! Can I carry something for you?"

"No, I'm fine. Listen, say what you've got to say, 'cause I'm late for my plane." Claire looked straight ahead as she talked, hurrying toward the now-empty loading door.

"I saw your interview with Ben Shaheed."

"Congratulations! You watch television!" she quipped.

"Listen, it really is important that I talk with you," Curran said.

"What did you have in mind?"

"Well," he said, desperation evident in his tone, "I don't think this is the place, and you're in a hurry. . . . Do you have a card so we could make an appointment?"

"How original, Lieutenant! You want my card."
She smiled knowingly.

"Hey, lady, I'm on the level here!" Curran looked
pleadingly at Claire. Suddenly, from out of nowhere, Hawkins fell in next to her on the other side.

"Let me explain what my partner is so inade-
quately trying to say. . . ." began Hawkins.

Curran grabbed his arm and said under his breath,
"GO AWAY!"

Hawkins smiled, patting him on the back. "Don't
worry!" he whispered over his shoulder, as he pulled
around in front of Claire Verens, causing her to stop.

"We have been assigned by the Inter-Agency Special Bureau to provide full escort services for the
duration of your stay in Washington. We have authorization to carry out—"

Claire heaved a sigh of disgust and pushed past
him. Curran grabbed him again and, through
clenched teeth said, "Hawk, will you take a walk!
This is business!"

Hawkins smiled and winked. "Sure, yeah, right!"

Claire reached the gate and showed her ticket to
the attendant. She looked back at Curran and Hawkins. "You two need to work on your act. The routine is pretty lame."

Curran looked offended. "Mine's no routine."

She smiled weakly and started to turn around.
"They never are. Well, gentlemen, unless you're going to Paris, your assignment is terminated."

Curran stuck his hand out and held her arm.
Hawkins stepped up as Curran and Claire looked at
each other, quietly sizing each other up. "We're serious," said Hawkins, conspiratorially.

Curran sighed deeply, giving Hawkins a drop-dead look. "He's not; I am."

Claire pulled her arm away and quickened her pace.

Hawkins leaned over to Curran and whispered hurriedly, "She's gettin' away, buddy! Let me handle this." He yelled after Claire as she turned and disappeared through the electronic-surveillance area, "Well, can we at least have your phone number?"

Curran dropped his head, exasperated. "You are one extraordinary DICKHEAD!"

Hawkins turned and stared at him in disbelief. "What did I do? I was just trying to help. Geez, what gratitude!" He shook his head and started walking up the ramp, back to their boarding gate.

Curran walked along behind him, shaking his head. "What did you think I was trying to do there, Hawk?"

"Boss," Hawkins turned back around, "it was obvious what you were trying to do. You were trying to pick her up! . . . And it wasn't working."

"No, Hawk, no!" Curran took Hawkins's face in both hands. "You asshole, I wasn't trying to pick her up! That's the journalist that interviewed Shaheed. I was trying to get some information on the guy."

Hawkins turned sheepish. "Well, shit! Why didn't you say so?"

"I didn't have a chance! My buddy here scared her off before I could ask her anything. Say . . . she wasn't bad-looking, was she?"

Hawkins began to laugh. "You're puttin' me on! You *were* hittin' on her!"

Smiling, Curran picked up his briefcase and walked onto the plane. "No, I really did want to talk to her. I just realized, after she walked away, that I liked the way she looked."

5

Large maps and diagrams were hanging from the briefing charts. Photographs lay scattered over the table, along with coffee cups, napkins, and a half-full box of donuts. Seated around the table, in the SEAL situation room were Curran, Hawkins, Graham, Ramos, Rexer, Dane, and Leary. Captain Dunne stood at the front of the table, holding a pointer.

"We've got satellite confirmation that the crates you saw in the shipyard have been transferred to the merchant ship *Latanya*. The *Latanya* departed yesterday for Tripoli, Lebanon." Dunne paused, as Curran looked up at him.

"How many hostiles are they reporting this time?" Curran asked.

Dunne shook his head. "We don't know how many hostiles are aboard, but there's another little wrinkle. The ship is also carrying Muslim pilgrims on the top deck, approximately a hundred."

"I just love it when civilians come along for the ride!" Ramos groaned.

Captain Dunne continued, "So if we pull a destroyer up alongside, we have a hostage problem. Therefore, gentlemen, your team is directed to interdict the ship at sea, neutralize any opposition—let's keep the blood on the bulkhead to a minimum—and secure the ship for boarding. The bomb boys get to grab some glory on this one."

Dunne turned and pointed to the map, tapping the end of the stick on the area marked "Mediterranean." He faced them, the pointer still on the map. "Your insertion platform is presently shadowing the *Latanya* in the eastern Mediterranean. . . ."

Around the table the men listened quietly, each aware of the hazards and pitfalls in the plan, but each glad they were getting a shot at recapturing the Stingers.

6

The sleek black attack submarine glided effortlessly under the dark waters of the eastern Mediterranean, the hypersonic propellers throbbing through the depths. Inside, Curran and Hawkins were slouched over a chart in the red-light glow of the sub. The sounding of the sonar drowned on in the background. The sub crew moved with easy confidence and skill inside the craft.

The captain of the submarine pulled away from the periscope eyepiece and turned to Curran. "There she is. Here, have a look."

Curran peered into the periscope at the rusted, sea-worn old freighter caught dead in the crosshairs of the scope. The *Latanya* was silhouetted across the night sky as it made its way along the surface. "That's her! Let's go!"

The rest of the SEALs were in the torpedo room, already dressed in their black wetsuits, busy either strapping on gear or studying the deck plan of the *Latanya*. Dane, finished with assembling his equipment, sat down on the floor, assumed the lotus position, and began to meditate. He closed his eyes and began to chant, a slow, steady "Ohmmm, Ohmmm," as he drifted deeper into his trance.

Leary fastened his fins to the strap at his waist. "What a nice night for a swim!" he said.

Rexer checked out his MP5K one more time. "Yeah, one of the many advantages of being a SEAL," he said. "Enjoying water sports, and the opportunity to travel to colorful, distant lands, meet interesting, exotic people,"—he strapped on the short black submachine gun—"and kill them."

Graham sat down next to Dane and opened his book, *Satanic Verses*. Leary walked over and squatted down next to him. "Hey, Graham, how come you always have your nose in a book?"

Graham looked up from the pages. "You know what they say: 'A mind is a terrible thing to waste.' "

Dane's eyes popped open. "I can think of a few minds I'd like to waste."

"I thought a hard-on was a terrible thing to waste," Rexer interjected.

"God knows, I've wasted a few!" Leary chimed in.

"I don't want to know!" Dane exclaimed.

Curran and Hawkins walked into the room. Curran clapped his hands together. "Okay, everybody, listen up. We'll all be engaged within the hour. Equipment check in thirty minutes, tops. Red goggles on now." The red goggles would preserve their night vision.

Forty-five minutes later they entered the lockout chamber, a narrow pressurization hull about the size of a shower stall. Rexer, the last to enter, lowered the bottom hatch. Curran looked around, making a quick last check, before hitting the speaker on the wall of the chamber.

"Bottom hatch is shut and dogged. Equalize to sea pressure."

A voice boomed out over the system: "Bottom hatch secure, aye. Equalize to sea pressure."

Water poured in, slowing rising up into the chamber. Hawkins raised his arm slightly, pretending to be bathing, and started singing. "Splish splash, I was takin' a bath, on about a Saturday night. . . ."

Dane laughed and joined in. "Rub dub, I was playin' in my tub, thinkin' everything was all right. . . ."

As the water reached midchest, the men lowered their face masks and made sure their regulators dropped onto their chests. The entire team, except for Curran, continued to sing until, one by one, their heads went underwater. Rexer, the tallest, strained his neck sideways and sang until the rising water forced him to stop. The water rose up over his head, and the only sound left in the chamber was the wheez of the regulators as the eight men waited in the cold, red-lit water.

An outside hatch opened against the smooth, black contour of the hull, and the eight SEALs began their ascent. They emerged on a calm sea, only recently disturbed by the *Latanya*'s wake. Graham broke the surface first. An inflated Zodiac popped up next to him, followed by Rexer and Dane. Curran and Hawkins surfaced, along with Leary and Ramos, on the other side of the hard-shelled, rubberized boat. Within a minute, a second Zodiac was inflated, and the SEALs boarded them, four men to a boat. The noiseless engines came to life, and the little boats cut through the water toward the freighter. Clouds covered the night sky, allowing little light for the men to work in but also concealing them in the darkness.

The old freighter rode heavily in the water. In a modern boat, this would indicate a weighty load, but in the *Latanya*'s case, it was just another indicator of age. The boat was badly maintained: there were only scattered patches of paint on the rusted hull.

The two Zodiacs quietly pulled alongside the stern and tucked in as close as possible. The SEALs waited in the boats as the first man in each of the crafts began the ascent up the side of the freighter.

Curran grabbed an outvalve drainpipe protruding from the hull and began his climb up the side. Hawkins, on the other side of the freighter, displayed his talent as a rock climber, picking his way to the top by using the screws and bolts that protruded from the rusted hull. The other SEALs in his group followed, inching slowly up the sheer hull like giant black arachnids.

First to the top, Curran's fingers curled over the edge of the deck near a lifeboat, while below him, the rest of his squad hung precariously to the side. He carefully pulled up and peered over the edge.

Curran's appearance over the edge of the deck aroused a young goat's curiosity. Standing near the main hatch, it stopped chewing on the root hanging from its mouth and lowered its head, making a threatening movement toward the intruder. When the man paid no attention to him, the goat looked away and continued to chew.

The deck was cluttered with people sleeping on the tops of the hatches, poor and destitute Muslim pilgrims who couldn't afford to travel with a roof over their heads. With them on top of the deck were their possessions—meager ragged bundles, a few goats, and some scrawny chickens.

After carefully scanning the sleeping people on the deck for any weapons or armed men, Curran turned his head to signal his men up, then froze.

Staring into Curran's face was an Al Shuhada sentry who had walked over to the edge of the boat to relieve himself. The man was fierce-looking; his hair seemed to spring out wildly in all directions from his head. He was as startled as Curran as he fumbled with his fly and brought up his AK47.

The man on deck definitely had the drop on him. Hanging by one hand, Curran made a frenzied attempt to pull the pistol from his belt. Before he could reach it, there were two dull thuds, and the Al Shuhada guard teetered forward with a grunt. The man fell over the rail at the davit, dropping past Curran and his men. He barely made a sound as he hit the water far below.

Curran watched in amazement, then pulled up over the side onto the deck. Hawkins stood on the deck, reholstering his silenced pistol, his squad behind him. Unfortunately, Curran noticed that familiar gleam in Hawkins's eyes again, the same edge-of-madness look he'd had at the refinery. Hawkins unslung his MP5 and stealthily began to move forward to the wheelhouse, as the rest of Curran's squad emerged on the deck and established their positions.

From a companionway on the portside, a sentry

stepped out and froze as he saw the men in black creeping nearer the wheelhouse. He snapped off the safety on his AK47 and raised the rifle to fire. Ramos and Leary saw him first and, with quick, silenced bursts, cut the man down in the passageway.

Hawkins reached the wheelhouse and yanked open the door, just as another of the Al Shuhada sentries reached to open it. Firing his weapon at point-blank range into the startled guard's chest, Hawkins caught the body on his rifle barrel and hurled him aside. He signaled his men to follow and charged inside, as Curran and his men entered from the opposite door.

Three Al Shuhada men, the freighter captain, and a helmsman were inside. The captain and the helmsman saw the black-clad gunmen first and dropped to the deck to avoid getting caught in a cross-fire. The Al Shuhada guards saw the men drop but, in the cramped little space, were unable to get their guns up and into action. They were quickly brought down by short bursts from Curran's silenced MP5.

The captain and his helper put their hands on their heads and began to plead in Arabic. Motioning for them to stay where they were, Curran spun around to Rexer and Leary.

"You two check below decks." He looked over at Graham and Ramos. "You secure the passengers. And stay alert!"

Hawkins began to herd the passengers toward the stern of the ship, where Graham and Ramos were searching each one at gun-point. One of the passengers screamed suddenly, and the crow parted to reveal an armed Al Shuhada guard. The terrorist grabbed a woman in front of him by the hair and put a Czech Scorpion machine pistol to her head.

The woman's eyes betrayed fear, but she stood very still while the gunman frantically looked for a way out. The terrorist had seen Hawkins but not Ramos and Graham, who were now moving into position on either side of him. Hawkins turned his rifle sideways and held it out, signaling nonaggression to the gunman. "I won't shoot!" Hawkins said to the Arab. The man warily edged closer to Hawkins, reaching over to take the MP5 from his hand, when Hawkins's foot lashed out, kicking the pistol from the terrorist's hand. He grabbed the man, pushing the woman to safety, and jabbed his own pistol into the man's chest. Caught, the Al Shuhada man raised his head defiantly and spat in Hawkins's face.

Hawkins jerked back with disgust, wiping his face on his shoulder. He glared at the Arab, who returned his stare. Finally, the Arab began to smile nervously and reached into his pocket. Hawkins fired three times, blasting him up against the wall. He seemed to hover in the air for a moment, his shocked face fixed on Hawkins, before he crumpled into a heap on the deck. Graham rushed over to the body and reached down to retrieve what was clasped in the man's hand. Turning around to Hawkins, he held out a small gold necklace.

Curran stood in the doorway and observed the scene. Hawkins saw him standing there and said, "We're full secure." The two men looked at each other in silence, and then Hawkins turned away.

Down in the hold compartment of the freighter, Rexer and Dane moved through the goods being shipped. Rexer reached down and ripped off a tarp hanging over three large crates. "Bingo!" he shouted to Dane. The metal crates all had "General Dynamics" marked on their sides.

Curran had crawled down into the hold, and he heard Rexer as he called out to Dane.

"That's it! Okay!" Curran said to Rexer and Dane. Then, into the mouthpiece on his headset: "Ballpoint, this is Bad Karma. Call in backup."

Within fifteen minutes, two large Navy helicopters were hovering over the deck as five explosive-ordinance-disposal technicians rappeled onto the hatch cover. The EOD officer landed next to Rexer, who helped him unhook the carabiner. Curran shouted over to the bomb team through the rotor blast, "Forward hold! Three crates!"

The ordinance officer gave him a thumbs-up and signaled his men to follow him. Together, they proceeded to the forward hold. Curran, Hawkins, Graham, and Dane followed close behind.

The EOD men quickly went about their work. Each man took a case and unlatched the metal lid. Sand began to pour out of the metal cases onto the freighter floor. One of the technicians reached down into the crate in front of him. He turned to Curran, letting sand sift down through his fingers. "You guys got took," he said.

"No!" Curran jumped over to the next one to look for himself. The box was filled with sand—simple, white sand.

7

Jim Elmore, Eliot West, Captain Dunne, and Lieutenant Curran were seated around a long, polished table covered with books and documents. Warren Stinson paced back and forth across the room, which was in the west wing of the White House.

Curran stared out the window as West spoke in a cool, dispassionate voice. "Ben Shaheed was ready for us. The freighter was a feint. No telling where those missiles are now."

Stinson stopped abruptly and, through clenched teeth, asked, "Why, damn it, don't we know where they are?"

West cleared his throat. "I believe I've said it before. It's priorities. We're underfunded and—"

Stinson glared at the man and slammed his fist onto the table. "Bullshit! Shaheed had better intel' than we did. He knew we were coming, and he set us up!"

Stinson gave a deep sigh of disgust and slumped

into his chair. The ticking of a clock on Stinson's desk was the only sound in the room.

"Well!" Stinson broke the silence after a few minutes. "Don't just sit there! I'll listen to anything—proposals, ideas, nutsy whims—anything!" He pointed to Dunne and Curran. "You guys are supposed to be experts on this sort of thing, for Christ's sake!" He glowered, growing more frustrated by the minute. He slammed his fist down on the table again, harder this time, sending papers flying. "I want those fucking missiles! Do you hear me? I want those missiles!" He was looking directly at Curran as he spoke.

The phone rang on his desk. Stinson jerked the receiver up to his ear, still looking at Curran as he answered. His expression abruptly changed. "Yes . . . yes, Mr. President . . . Yes, Elmore and West are here with me. . . . Sure. We're on our way." He hung up and stood. "That's it for today. I'll talk with you people later. Let's get a plan going here—quickly!"

Chair legs scraped against the wooden floors as the people around the table stood up, gathering their papers. Elmore and West waited at the door as Stinson turned to Dunne and Curran. "Get back with me!" he said as he joined the others and started down the corridor to the president's office.

Curran and Dunne stepped out into the sunshine and began to walk down Pennsylvania Avenue. Curran was silent, his face drawn and worried.

"He's talking out his ass!" Dunne said as he walked along. "It's not your responsibility to gather and analyze information."

"Oh, that's fine with me. He must know that I want those missiles a helluva lot worse than he does." Curran kicked at an imagined stone on the sidewalk.

"So what next? Go over to Langley and start reading dispatches?" Dunne asked.

"It's a start."

"Look, James," Dunne said affectionately, "you're taking this personally." They walked on a while, before Dunne spoke again. "I'm ordering you and your team to stand down."

Curran stopped walked and turned to face the captain. "Now wait a minute, sir, I—"

Interrupting him, Dunne said, "Don't argue with me, Lieutenant! It's just for a day or two. . . . You and the team need to relax; just chill out. Get a clear perspective."

"I . . ." Curran sputtered.

"That's an order." Dunne's face was like stone.

"Yes, sir," Curran's jaw snapped as he saluted his commander.

8

A football hurtled through the air. Dane's long arm shot forward, snatching the ball in midflight. He pulled the ball close to his chest and started to run, when he was suddenly slammed to the ground by Rexer.

"Ughhh!" he grunted, as he hit the sand hard and the football flew out of his hands.

Graham reached down, grabbed the free ball, and whirled around to throw it, coming face-to-face and body-to-body with Hawkins. They collided, falling to the ground and grappling for the ball. Leary wrested the ball away and handed off to Dane.

Dane faded back and made a long pass to Ramos, who lateraled back to Graham. Rexer was pass-protecting, and he wiped out three oncoming rushers with a full-extension body block. Graham slung the ball about twenty yards in the air to a sprinting Hawkins, who, in a last desperate move, climbed up the back of his defender, lunged with one arm, and snagged the ball, wrapping it tightly to his chest as he fell over the imaginary goal line. Back on his feet, he whooped and spiked the ball to the ground. Throwing his hands up over his head, he ran victoriously up the beach until he reached two attractive women stretched out on beach towels.

"Did you see that play!" he asked, catching his breath. "Did you see it! Velcro hands! All State! All WORLD! The NFL Play of the Week!" Hawkins collapsed between the girls. "I never cease to amaze myself. . . . You DID see that catch, right?"

Both girls turned toward him, staring blankly. The brunette in the deeply cut black suit wiped sand off her arm. "Just who the hell are you?"

Hawkins smiled. "I'm glad you asked—"

"Hey, Hawk!" Graham called. "Are you still in the game?"

Looking over his shoulder, Hawkins shouted, "No, I've got to save myself for Monday night. Thanks for the scrimmage, fellows. I'll get you some free tickets to the Big One!" He turned back around to the curious faces of his new fans. "Say," he said, looking from the redhead's barely concealed breasts into her bright green eyes, "you and your friend aren't football fans, are you?"

Exchanging looks, the girls both shook their heads. Hawkins beamed. "Hey, that's all right with me! I need a break from all that fan chatter anyway. I'm down here relaxing before the Super Bowl."

Both girls began to talk excitedly. "No! No! I'm relaxing—no talk about football!" Hawkins said dramatically. "Besides, I'm more interested in you two."

Rexer had been standing close enough to hear the

exchange. He shook his head and laughed as he walked up to join the others.

"What's going on?" Dane asked as Rexer neared him.

"Hawkins is about to score, but it won't be in this game," Rexer said, still laughing. "He's got those two convinced that he's a pro."

"Oh, he's a pro, all right . . . a super pro!" Ramos said. "Let's go get some brewskis and kick back."

Rexer and Dane joined him on the beer run to the store while the others unloaded coolers of food on the beach. Graham pulled some firewood out of the back of his trunk and dragged it down the sand.

As they went about their business, Hawkins busily snowstormed the scantily clad ladies down the beach.

The sun was beginning to set as Rexer lit the fire. Within a few minutes, the logs were crackling and spitting. Flames of orange, blue, and green shot up into the air, shedding light on the figures gathered around.

Graham had gone back up to his car and returned to the fireside, a guitar in his hands. He settled down in the sand, facing the fire, and began to strum the instrument. "Hey, come on everybody! 'You are my sunshine, my only sunshine, you make me happy . . .' Hey, nobody's singing!"

The team members, now joined by some of their girls, were stone silent, staring rays of death at Graham.

"Okay, so you don't know that song. . . . Any requests?" he asked.

"Yeah, do you know how to play 'Over the Dunes and Far, Far Away'?" Leary yelled out. The others laughed as Graham first looked puzzled, then recognized the insult.

"You peasants! You have no appreciation for music!" He turned his back to them and continued to strum the guitar for his own pleasure.

Curran sat over to the side, away from the others. Tablet in hand, he was busily scribbling down notes, oblivious to the noise and people around him. His brow was furrowed in deep concentration.

Hawkins ambled up the dunes to the fire, a girl on each arm. "Hello! Meet my two new best friends, Nicole and Renee."

Dane looked them over. "You two French?"

"Only when asked," the redhead answered.

A whoop of laughter went up. Hawkins stood there proudly exhibiting his new conquests, when something in the distance caught his eye. In the parking lot at the ridge above the sand, a policeman was sticking a ticket on the windshield of his red GTO. "Oh well," Hawkins muttered to himself, "one more for the collection."

Graham stood up, laying the guitar on the sand, and yelled out to the figure walking toward them on the beach. "Hi, babe, I didn't think you'd get off in time to join us."

Jolena, in jeans and a white V-neck sweater, waved back. "Yeah, we weren't busy, so Al let me off early." She made a stop by Hawkins. "You're not supposed to talk to Graham until after Saturday," she said, not totally serious but not smiling, either.

"Well . . . now, WHAT could be happening Saturday?" Hawkins teased.

"None of your damn business, that's for sure!"

Jolena faced him, pushing her hands deep into her pockets.

"Hey, Graham," Hawkins called over his shoulder, "we're still on locked and cocked alert. Aren't you risking a lot by setting a date in three days?"

"Believe me, Hawk, he'd be risking a lot more if he didn't," she said, as she walked over and sat down by Graham.

"Oh, Jolena, dearest, I believe it," Hawkins said. He spotted Curran sitting off to the side. "Hey, boss, where were you today? You've never missed a post-op blow-out."

"I've been up at Langley, lookin' for some answers," Curran said, continuing to write.

Hawkins led the giggling girls over to where Curran was sitting. "This is a party, Curran . . . and I've got just the girl for you."

Curran looked up as Hawkins glanced from one girl to the other and back again. He shrugged his shoulders. "Sorry, boss, I can't give either one up!" Curran smiled and returned to his notes.

"Now, what were we . . . Oh yes! . . . Well, this football-star thing is only deep cover for my CIA activities. . . . You're not going to tell anyone this, are you?" Hawkins led the girls off toward the parking lot. As they walked up to the cars, a tow truck was pulling the GTO up a ramp onto a flatbed carrier.

Hawkins dropped his arms from around the girls. "Oh, shit!" he cried as he started running, trying to overtake the now-moving tow truck. The two girls squealed and hurried along after him.

Watching the commotion, the SEALs on the beach

83

burst into laughter as Hawkins hauled ass down the beachfront street, the girls running along behind.

Several hours passed, with the team and their dates enjoying the fire and the evening. The logs burned down to coals, emitting a comfortable warmth against the cool breeze blowing in off the ocean.

Graham was stretched out on his side, warming his back by the fire, a book in his hands and Jolena curled up beside him.

Curran, sitting near them, put down his notes and stared intently into the fire, while Jolena talked.

"So I start planting petunias and begonias for the Norfolk Nursery tomorrow. My boy here"—she reached over and squeezed Graham's leg as she spoke—"never did think much of me slinging pitchers of beer. Guess he didn't like telling his buddies that his fiancée was a barmaid."

Graham glanced up from his book. "She's a genius with plants," he said with pride.

Curran smiled as he watched them. He secretly envied Graham. Jolena wasn't a beauty, but she loved him, and he had her to talk to. They had a special kind of caring and understanding. And they needed each other. That was something Curran had known about them from the start.

"Can I depend on you to deliver Graham on Saturday?" Jolena asked as she snuggled closer to her man.

"You know this business, Jolena, but we're about ninety-seven percent of the way there," Curran answered.

Jolena smiled a confident smile, "Okay, but if that

three percent pops up, I'll guarantee you'll be short one great SEAL!"

"We'll be there. Say, Graham, what were you reading?" Curran strained to see the book.

"Here, you can have it—I'm finished." Graham handed the book over to him. Curran flinched as he looked at the cover. It was *Tears of Rage: Inside the Mind of a Terrorist*, by Claire Verens. He flipped it over. There on the back was the picture of the woman he'd chased down the ramp at the airport. He barely heard Jolena speaking.

"And you make sure your friend Hawkins keeps his bullshit to himself!" she was saying with some finality.

Slipping the book into his pocket, Curran shook his head and patted Jolena on the shoulder. "Look, you can't take him seriously. He's crazy about both of you. Believe it or not, beneath all that shuck and jive is a decent—"

He was interrupted by the loud roar of a deep-throated engine, loud, shrieking laughter, and the sound of a siren.

Blasting down the beach, rooster tails of sand flying in the air, was a red GTO manned by Hawkins, flanked by his two screaming girls. As they disappeared into the distance, Jolena said, "As you were saying . . ."

9

The gallery of the Senate hearing room was filled to capacity. Claire Verens was seated at a table in front of a bank of microphones. She wore a pale salmon-colored tailored suit. Her hair was pulled back into a neat bun at the nape of her neck. Incongruously, a pencil was stuck in her hair and protruded out behind her ear. She leaned toward the mike to answer the question.

"Yes, I do think covert actions are sometimes necessary, as long as the operational elements are not given free rein."

Facing her was a full complement of senators and congressmen with their aides, all seated at a circular rostrum. The pinched face of the senior congressman from Texas leaned forward and asked, rather testily, "The terrorists have free rein, Miss Verens. Don't you think the rules should be the same for both sides?"

Claire hesitated for a minute, then said, "We've

seen too many cases where these operations have gotten out of control—"

"Yes," interrupted the congressman, "I'll take the risk of the occasional slip-up if it resulted in the elimination of terrorism."

Claire leaned farther into the mike. "Sir, this is a nation of laws. Laws, according to the Constitution, to be obeyed by every single citizen of this country . . . with NO exceptions." She continued to stare intently at the congressman, who looked down at his notes and began to fidget under her intense gaze.

A great silence filled the hearing room, until the chairman, a senator from Georgia, spoke into the microphone. "Thank you, Miss Verens. Your expertise in this matter and your articulate and frank responses have been deeply appreciated." With this, he slammed down the gavel. "The Joint Subcommittee on Terrorism and Covert Response will recess until two o'clock."

Claire gathered up her notes, slipping them into a small tan briefcase. The standing-room-only gallery behind her began to empty out. She joined the crowd at the door and made her way out into the hallway.

Curran stood by the door, waiting for her as she emerged. She started down the corridor, moving toward the outside doors. Curran took several long strides and appeared at her elbow. "Excuse me."

She turned to look at him, vaguely recognizing him. "Do I know you?" she asked, without stopping.

Curran smiled sheepishly, "Dulles Airport."

Claire groaned. "Oh, God, please, I don't have time for this!"

"I'm not trying to pick you up. I just want to talk to you," Curran pleaded.

"Tell me again," she said, continuing down the hall. "What do you want to know?"

Curran stepped in front of her, making her stop. "Information about Ben Shaheed and the Al Shuhada. I've read your book. I need to know more."

She looked at him with mild curiosity. "Like what?" she asked.

"Anything. How you went about your research, details you thought weren't important enough to include in the book. Outtakes from your interview, maybe . . ." He was wound up, trying to convey his urgency to her.

"Maybe where you could locate him? . . . Isn't that what this is about?" She stared at him, distrust building in her eyes.

"There's more to it than that," Curran answered.

"There always is," she said with disgust. "Now, will you get out of my way."

Frustrated, Curran continued to stand in front of her, blocking her escape. "No, please. I don't think you understand."

"I understand all too well. Who is it this time? The CIA, Israeli Intelligence, the NSC, Naval Intelligence? Who do you represent?" she asked, her voice brittle with anger.

"I'm a Navy SEAL."

Claire looked at the man in front of her as if she'd never seen him before. He was in civilian clothes—tan slacks and a tweed blazer. His hair was clipped close, what there was of it, and it was dark brown, the same color as the eyes that were blazing with an intensity that made her uncomfortable. He was slender and angular, but she sensed that he had great physical strength. "A SEAL!" She laughed. "Now they send a SEAL?"

"Nobody sent me. I came on my own."

"Look . . . SEAL . . . do you know the importance to a journalist of protecting a source's confidentiality?" she asked.

Curran started to answer, but she cut him off. "Don't give me that tired old saw about higher principles and for the good of the whole, 'cause I'm not buying it! You can't reduce matters to mean your ethics are superior to mine." She was getting wound up for a knockout blow.

"I don't believe," Curran said softly, "that I said anything."

"I'm well versed in anticipating these comments." She began to back down a little, to soften. He was staring at her again, but there was something new in the look. It made her more uncomfortable than his earlier intensity.

"You know something?" he asked finally, his lips beginning to curve into an easy smile. "You remind me of my ex-wife."

"What!" Claire was now concerned that she may have encountered a madman in the hall.

"And do you know something else?" He stepped closer to her. "You have a pencil sticking out of your hair."

Claire reached up and felt the pencil. "Oh, shit!" She pulled it out, obviously mortified.

Curran continued to smile at her. "Don't worry about it. CSPAN only has a viewer base of about a million and a half. Other than that, you look fine."

She started to say something to him, faltered,

then walked toward the door. With her hand on the handle, she stopped, turned around slowly, and walked back to him.

"Okay, so I'm curious. Why is a SEAL so desperate to find out about Ben Shaheed?"

The smile disappeared as if it had never been there, replaced by a look devoid of emotion. "It's part of our job to profile all known terrorists."

"That's a bullshit answer. I'll be at this address tomorrow." She pulled a piece of paper from her briefcase and hurriedly wrote on it. She handed it to him, turned on her heels, and walked out through the doors.

The taxi pulled up to the steps of the Library of Congress. Curran stepped out, threw some money to the cabbie and closed the door. In his left hand he held a small package. Taking two steps at a time, he bounded up the stairs and through the doors into the building.

An aide guided him through labyrinthian canyons of books. Finally, the guide pointed to a tiny study cubicle. Curran thanked the guide, took a deep breath, and knocked on the door.

"Come in."

He opened the door and stepped into the small room. The table had several books stacked neatly at one end, a Toshiba T1000 laptop computer, and some three-by-five note cards. Claire was seated at the table, making notes on the cards, as he walked in. She gave him a curious look as she peered up over her reading glasses.

"Here." He handed her the package. "Peace offering," he said, in answer to the questioning look she gave him.

She opened the package and pulled out a carton of fifty number-two pencils. Instinctively, her hand flew up to her hair. She grinned self-consciously for a minute, then said, "Thanks for the pencils. . . . But I can't be bribed."

"That wasn't the idea, but do you mind if I sit?" he said, looking around for a chair.

"Where?" Claire watched him as he smiled and sat down on the floor next to her.

The tiny cubicle seemed to grow smaller, forcing a kind of intimacy and quiet tension. They stared at each other wordlessly, neither one able to turn away or blink.

"Okay," Curran said, "will you hear me out before arguing against points I haven't made?"

"I'm all ears," she said, offering none of the resistance Curran was expecting. He was thrown off a bit, but he regained his control and started.

"First of all, I'm not going to ask you to violate any professional ethics. All I want is information about matters that could affect myself and my team in the future."

Claire laughed. "The future! Who do you think you're talking to here?"

He focused on her eyes, holding them captive as he spoke. "I am very much aware of who I'm talking to."

She tapped a pencil on the tabletop nervously, then realized she was doing it and stopped. "Let's see. You're most likely a member of SEAL Team, a unit set up specializing in counterterrorist tactics, and most likely you were part of the recent rescue operation in the Mideast and probably had a first-hand experience with Ben Shaheed himself. Am I right so far?"

"You're always so far ahead of me, I don't think I even need to be around for us to have a conversation." Curran smiled his warmest smile.

She raised an eyebrow while she studied him, then said, "All right, I'll do it."

"Do what?" he asked.

"What you just asked me. I'll brief you." She assumed a businesslike pose and added, "That is, if we can work out a *quid pro quo* arrangement. I want to learn about the SEALs."

Curran looked confused. "Like what?" he asked.

"Oh, like what your role was in Honduras, Nicaragua, Libya, Grenada, Lebanon, the *Achille Lauro* . . . how and when you're deployed, and exactly how much of a threat a secret commando unit poses to a democratic society."

Curran just smiled back at her. "And, of course, what the SEALs have up their sleeves concerning the Al Shuhada," she added.

"Ms. Verens, I'd be glad to tell you all I know . . . as long as it's not classified," Curran said. "When can we start?"

"Well, Counterterrorist, I've got a pretty heavy schedule for the next two weeks. Say . . . three weeks from today?" She leafed through an appointment calendar.

"Won't work. I don't have that kind of time. It's ten o'clock now," he said, looking at his watch. "What about starting at two o'clock?"

"What? You mean two o'clock today?"

"I know that's pushing you, but I'm pushed, too.

If you can't do it, I'll have to go elsewhere." There was no doubt in Claire's mind that he meant it.

"Elsewhere? Who else has the information you're looking for?" she asked, smiling.

"I don't know. Someone. I don't have time for games any more. I'm sorry if you didn't think I was serious." He stood up, getting ready to leave the little room.

"Look, I'm not sure we're going to be able to help each other, but I'm willing to try. Let me make a few calls. I'll clear tomorrow, and we can talk." There was something about the way he looked that made her aware of his urgency.

"No, I don't know where I'll be tomorrow. And I'm not giving you a line. I've got a major problem, and I'm not sure where the answer is. I thought you might know. Thanks anyway." He opened the door and stepped out.

Claire sat there, puzzled and surprised that he had left. Her instincts said to call him back, to help him, but it wouldn't have been the first time her instincts had lied. "Oh, shit!" she said aloud to the empty room as she sprang from her chair and hit the door. She could barely see him, walking quickly down one of the corridors of books.

"Lieutenant," she said in a conversational tone. He was still moving away from her. "LIEUTENANT!" she shouted, her voice surprising her by its loudness.

He stopped and turned around. There was no hope on his face, no look of triumph, just curiosity. "Yes?" he said, still standing there.

"God help me . . . I think maybe you're real. Let's talk. Pick me up at three o'clock, but I can't cancel anything past today. The address is 477 Standish, number twelve. It's a place I rent here in Washington."

"I'll be there. Dress casual—we'll be traveling light. . . . And, thanks." He smiled and turned back around, continuing down the corridor to the exit.

Claire needed a great deal of charm to clear her appointment book for the day. The rescheduling of the canceled appointments made a living hell out of the rest of her week. She sat out on her patio, for the first time since she had rented the place the previous year, looking at the view of the golf course. It was two-forty. She had finished her calls and changed into some jeans and a red-and-blue striped rugby shirt. She was toying with the idea of taking a tape recorder with her when the intercom buzzed.

"Yes?" she said as she pressed the button on the wall.

"Hi! Lieutenant Curran here. Are you ready?"

"Yes. Did you want to come up first?" She waited for his answer.

"Thanks, but we have some ground to cover. Perhaps some other time."

"Okay, I'll be right down." She was surprisingly disappointed by his answer.

"Hi. You might need a hat," he said, as she met him at the foot of the stairs. "I've got the top off the jeep, and it's a little windy."

"No problem—I've got a hat in my jacket," Claire said, whipping out a baseball cap and pushing her hair up inside. "I forgot to ask: Where are we going?"

95

"I thought I'd show you some of the training we go through, the conditioning. You said you wanted to know about the SEALs . . . see how we live; then you might understand us." He ushered her out to his jeep and opened the door for her as she got in.

"You don't have to do that," she said, settling into the bucket seat. "I can open my own door."

"Hey, I'm sorry. No offense meant. I'm from the old South, and my mama would roll over in her grave if I didn't open the door for a lady." He had a big honest face, and she liked his open smile.

He's either the best phony you've ever met, or the guy is on the level, Claire thought as they pulled out of her parking lot.

"Where is the training area?"

"Just down the road a piece and then back to the beach. You'll enjoy this, I think," Curran answered.

10

Curran looked at his watch while they sat waiting for the light to change. He had been early—about twenty minutes early. She had every reason to feel pushed: He was, in fact, pushing her. He was pleasantly surprised that she had been ready, and he would have loved to have gone up to her apartment, but the stand-down time was running out. And somewhere out there were five Stinger missiles in the control of a man who was prepared to die for his cause.

"Hey, are you always early?" Curran asked as the light changed.

"You told me you were short on time. I don't want to waste any. I live on a tight schedule myself."

"Well, I appreciate your making time for me. You said you wanted to know about the SEALs. I thought we would go out and watch the team train."

"Do not welch on me, Lieutenant. I don't just want to watch you train, I want to know what you've done after the training was over!" She pulled at the blue baseball cap, trying to push up an escaped strand of hair.

"I'm going to do just what I promised to do." Curran liked the frankness of this woman and her attitude. She was all business, even a little flinty, but easy to be around.

They pulled through the gates of the training area. A guard saluted Curran and waved them through. The SEAL training area was a large fenced-in compound near the Naval base. A Sea King helicopter swooped overhead as they drove down the dirt road toward a large open field. Curran stopped the jeep by the side of the road behind an ambulance and looked over at Claire.

"This is a good place to start. Have you ever seen a rapppeling action from a helicopter?" he asked, getting out of the jeep.

She shook her head as she opened her door and jumped easily to the ground. Curran pointed up to the Sea King that began to circle over them. The chopper came in low, less than forty feet off the ground. A rope came tumbling out the door and dropped down, clearing the ground by a few feet. The first of eight men started down the rope, quickly followed by another, then another, until all eight men were either on the rope or had completed the drop. As they dropped off, they made a neat roll to the ground and came up on their feet.

The chopper pulled off and flew over the horizon to pick up another group as the first bunch walked over to a truck and climbed into the back.

Claire watched in amazement: They all seemed so casual about it. "How often do the people on the team have to do this?"

"We have to practice every day, to refine techniques and to maintain mental sharpness," Curran replied.

The chopper made another pass, and eight more men began their rapid descent down the swaying rope. Claire was struck with the top physical condition of these men and their professionalism. "I'm impressed," she said, as Curran looked over her way.

"You've got more to see. Let's go." Curran guided her back to the jeep through the swirling clouds of dust kicked up by the low-flying chopper.

They could still hear the *wop-wop-wop* of the chopper as they drove away. Three miles up the road, they parked at a small dock. A Zodiac was awaiting them, Rexer standing at the controls. "Afternoon, Lieutenant," he said, with unaccustomed formality, as Curran and Claire approached the boat.

"Ms. Verens, meet Alex Rexer, one of the men on my team. Rexer, Ms. Verens is an expert on Ben Shaheed." Curran held her arm as she stepped into the rubber boat.

Rexer nodded to her and started the soundless engine on the boat. He turned to Curran. "You wanted to watch the drownproofing, right, sir?"

"Affirmative."

"Drownproofing? What's that?" Claire asked, her eyes wide with curiosity.

"Well, we're almost there, so let me explain quickly as we get in a position to watch," Curran answered.

Their Zodiac pulled up alongside another Zodiac about a quarter of a mile offshore. Claire watched as SEALs, their feet and hands bound, were thrown over the side of the other boat into the ocean. "My

God!" she exclaimed. "What kind of sadistic game is this?"

"This is no game, it's deadly serious," Curran answered. "It's all part of getting a SEAL to the point that the water becomes first nature, not second nature."

"How many do you drown before they get to that point?"Claire was getting worried, when suddenly the first of the men popped to the surface, followed by the others, and they started climbing back into the boat.

"They have to be prepared for all contingencies. If we have to infiltrate, sabotage, and blow up targets, we have to be ready to go anywhere, at any time, and under any conditions. It's also a mental test, to reaffirm that they can get out of almost any situation if they don't panic." The last of the SEALs pulled themselves back over the side of the boat as Curran was speaking.

"Sabotage, infiltrate? *Covert* operations?" Claire looked at Curran, watching his eyes as she spoke.

"*Clandestine* operations. We're trained to respond to the kind of war we expect to be fighting in the 1990s—low-intensity guerrilla wars and acts of terrorism." Curran avoided looking at her by staring intently at the men in the boat. He glanced over at Rexer, who was studying the woman in the baseball cap. "Rexer, let's go back in now."

The Zodiac turned slowly and began its trip back to shore.

"You were there, weren't you? You've been in the Middle East?" Claire ran her hands over the jacket on her lap, then flipped her eyes up into Curran's.

"Beirut."

"In '84, right?" she snapped, a hound with her fox on the run.

Curran smiled uneasily. "Right," he said, as they pulled up to the dock. "Let's move on."

"Love to!" she said, jumping from the boat before either Rexer or Curran could offer her a hand. "Where to next?"

Rexer turned his back so that Claire couldn't see him and said under his breath to Curran, "Nice, sir, real nice!" Curran stared back at him, as if not understanding, and stepped over onto the dock.

"I thought we'd go watch the snipers." He waved at Rexer and started up the dock behind Claire. He noticed that she walked with confidence—no exaggerated sway to the hips; just the smooth, gliding movements of a jungle cat.

Dane was at the range, bench-resting a huge sniper rifle sighted on the targets far off in front of him as they walked up.

"This is Dane—J. R. Dane. That rifle of his has laser-, starlight-, and thermal-sight systems. It fires ball, armor-piercing, incendiary, or explosive .50-caliber rounds at ranges up to two miles." There was a touch of pride in Curran's voice as he spoke. "Dane is considered to be one of the best snipers we have."

"Pick a yuppie," Dane said in greeting.

"A what?" Claire asked, thinking that maybe she had misunderstood the strange, hollow-eyed man stretched out in front of her.

"A target," Curran explained. "When Dane was in training, he couldn't hit the broad side of a barn, but he had the right psychological profile: cool, calm, good reflexes. His instructor was determined to improve his marksmanship, so he told him to imagine the targets were something that he hated."

"I hate yuppies," Dane said, sounding a bit like the H.A.L. computer in *2001*.

"I, uh, I see." Claire moved back a pace or two.

"See that?" Dane pointed to an old car body in the field some hundred yards away.

"Yeah," Claire said. "That doesn't look too hard."

"Not that car," Dane said, mildly frustrated but still speaking in his monotone. "That one, there; fifteen hundred meters." He pointed in the direction. Curran handed Claire a set of protective earphones as he donned his own.

Claire followed Dane's finger and looked across the field. "Is that a car?" she asked, squinting to focus.

Dane fired the rifle. Without a silencer, it sent out a muzzle flash five feet wide and a report like a thunderclap. "Not any more." He smiled.

"Impressive!" uttered Claire, obviously taken aback by the blast. She pulled off the earphones.

"Maybe you'll understand why we call him God," Curran said, more than a little pleased with Dane's shot.

"Do SEALs use Stinger missiles?" The question sounded so innocent as it escaped her lips.

Curran felt an involuntary shiver pass over him. "No." He paused and recomposed himself. "Why?"

Claire took note and said, casually, "The day we met at the committee hearing, I visited the SEAL headquarters. I noticed a large section of the bulletin board in your office plastered with pictures of Stingers."

Curran was shaken, but his outward appearance

betrayed nothing. "You were over there? How interesting . . . Well, it's our job to be familiar with all types of weaponry. We have more to see. Are you interested?"

"Very! Lead on, Lieutenant," she said, satisfied that she had ruffled his cool exterior.

They walked into a large concrete silo that dwarfed the figures inside. Claire, Curran, and another group made up mostly of colonels gathered around a huge glass window, through which could be seen a simulated ship's hull. Several SEALs ascended a circular staircase to join other specklike figures at the top of the tall dive tank.

"They have to dive from sixty-five feet," Curran explained. "Our top guys go first to set the pace for the others to beat. This is a free dive—no oxygen, no decompression devices."

Claire watched in amazement as two figures swam into view in the window and started to work.

"What are they doing?" She pointed to the men swimming in front of them.

"They're setting simulated explosives by attaching and tying demolition knots to the ship's hull," Curran answered. "Notice that they're not wearing tanks. This has to be done on one breath of air."

One of the figures slowly pivoted around in the water and swam up to the window, planting a big kiss on the glass.

"Don't tell me! It's the Creature from the Black Lagoon!" Claire exclaimed, watching the man make his ascent.

Curran groaned. "Almost that bad. That's Hawkins. He's part fish, the team's number-one diver. He claims he can tie his cords and play a game of five-card stud before he needs air. He's hard to control, but he's good, real damn good. He'll have my job soon."

"Is he coming on that strong, or are you thinking of stepping down?" Claire asked, watching Curran.

Curran hadn't expected the question. He peered deeply into her dark eyes, noticing the golden flecks within the brown depths. "Maybe; maybe both. Come on. Let's go before he presses something else on the glass."

They left the silo and drove to the beach again, where there were several SEALs in pairs on the marked course, swimming in the rough ocean around the breakwater.

Claire remained seated in the jeep as Curran came around and opened her door. "Thanks," she said, allowing him to help her to the ground.

The SEALs were breaking through the waves, back to the beach, where they alternated, carrying each other fifty yards at a time. Loud pyrotechnic charges were going off around them as they jumped into mud-filled ditches, assembled AK47s, and fired a few rounds. This done, they began to move up a mine-marked hill to a platform, where they pulled up into the breech of a hovering Sea Knight helicopter.

"Our basic training and winnowing-out process is done on Coronado Island. By the time we get through that six-month period we affectionately call hell, we can do whatever we're called on to do. Only one in a hundred makes it," explained Curran, watching the panorama before him. "The training weeds out those who might quit. For a SEAL, endurance is everything. You just never give up. Ever."

Claire had been observing the SEALs as they trained, but she stopped as Curran spoke, studying him.

"Thanks, Lieutenant." She added slowly, "This is all very interesting, but what I want to learn about the SEALs goes a lot deeper than the standard VIP tour."

"Okay, maybe we could negotiate matters over dinner this evening." Curran helped her back into the jeep.

"Maybe . . . All right, I'll look forward to it, Lieutenant."

"Please, drop the 'Lieutenant' business, Ms. Verens." He held the door open a moment before closing it.

"Okay, then call me Claire," she said, getting the same uneasy feeling she had felt before with him, but this time enjoying it.

"Fine. Claire it is. Call me James."

"No, no, I think I prefer calling you Curran. If you'll drop me off, I'll meet you someplace."

"I could wait for you to change." Curran continued to gaze steadily at her.

"Thank you, but I'd rather meet you." She stiffened her back as she spoke and slid back in her seat.

"As you wish, Claire. Say eight o'clock at the Trident Bar. Then we'll go get something to eat. You like seafood, don't you?"

"Yes, I like seafood, and I know where the Trident is. I'll be there at eight."

They drove back to her apartment in an uncomfortable silence. Occasionally she would ask a specific question about the SEAL training she had witnessed, and Curran would answer, crisply and precisely. The warmth between them seemed to have disappeared as she stepped out of the jeep. Curran had serious doubts as to whether she would keep the date.

11

The crowd at the Trident sounded louder than usual. Curran questioned his judgment in having invited Claire to meet him there. In fact, Curran questioned his judgment in several areas, all of them personal. Since he'd dropped Claire off, he had become quite retrospective.

He had been married once, sort of. He had been too young; she had been too young. Neither one of them had tried to compromise. After two years of a mutually miserable existence, they agreed that it was a mistake. Now, as Curran waited for Claire to arrive, he realized how little he had tried to make it work.

The realization was sharp, sudden, and painful. He knew that whatever he and his wife originally shared had been destroyed, never to be regained. Still, he missed the warmth; he longed for someone to come home to, to come home for. It had been easy for a while. He immersed himself in the SEAL team, filling every empty hour with study or practice; but lately, there had been hours he couldn't fill—empty, meaningless hours. He was also aware that he hadn't had a date—a planned, arranged date—in a long time.

He shook his head and leaned on the bar. He needed to get a grip here. Claire Verens was no date, she was business, strictly business. He wanted to get to Ben Shaheed and the Stingers, and Verens was the most direct path—if he could get her cooperation, and that was a very big *if*.

Curran jumped as Graham clapped him on the back. "Hey, boss! Let me get us a round." Graham signaled for the waiter and ordered two ryes before Curran could object.

"I'm glad you're here. Jolena is meeting me in a minute and I really need to get a few things clear." The waiter returned with the drinks and Graham took a sip from his.

"But first"—Graham grinned at Curran—"I saw you today over on the beach. With that Verens woman."

"I was just escorting her around the training area. She expressed an interest in the SEALs." Curran tried to look disinterested.

"SEALs or SEAL? You know, I thought about this a lot before I came over here tonight. She's right for you, boss. Well-educated, classy-looking! You know, you might just explore the possibilities." Graham enjoyed watching Curran squirm for a change.

"Drop it. She is strictly business. Now," Curran said, changing the subject, "what's this you need to get straight before Jolena gets here?"

"Well," Graham asked with a frown, "do you think I'm doing the right thing?"

"Oh, come on, Graham! Everything's fine. You love her, she loves you. It's okay," Curran said, taking a sip of his drink.

"Yeah." Graham shook his head in agreement, then paused. "But we come from such different backgrounds."

Curran, fighting his own problem, began becoming less than sympathetic. "Let it go, Graham. You know, as much as I love you, you're beginning to piss me off."

Graham twisted around to face Curran. "Sorry," he said, really meaning it. He continued to twitch around, wrestling with his problem; then he blurted out what was on his mind: "Just one thing: . . . Ever since I got engaged, women—beautiful women— have been popping up everywhere . . . and they're *available*."

Curran looked startled. "You must be hallucinating. You have been under a lot of pressure." Curran put his arm around Graham's shoulders and patted him on the arm. "Billy Graham, you have the ability to overwork a problem. Basic fact is you want to marry Jolena, right?"

"Well . . ." Graham hesitated. "Yes! I mean, she's so beautiful!"

Curran glanced over at him with amazement, then looked back into his drink.

"I mean," continued Graham, "she's the best thing that ever happened to me. She doesn't mind that I'm a SEAL. In fact, she's proud of me."

"Then don't let her get away. She's a good woman, and you are one lucky man." Curran finished his drink and looked up in the bar mirror. "OH SHIT!" he said, seeing Hawkins approach them.

"Let me let you guys buy me a drink," Hawkins said, joining them at the bar. He twirled one of the seats next to Graham and then sat on it, letting it take him halfway around on its spin.

"You know, Hawk," Graham said nervously, "I'm not supposed to talk to you until after the wedding."

Hawkins laughed. "You mean to tell me you let that—"

"That WHAT, Hawkins?" Jolena interrupted, as she walked up to the men.

Hawkins never missed a beat. "Why, that charming, sweet, warm, and wonderful fiancée of yours. That's what I was going to say, Jolena honey. Now, aren't you embarrassed?"

She gave him a look that would melt steel, then glanced over at Curran. "Roll up your pants, Curran—it's too late to save your shoes! You," she said to Graham, "come with me."

Graham grinned and shrugged as he got up and left with her.

Hawkins turned around and looked at Curran. "Why James!" he said, in mock amazement. "Don't you look pretty tonight! You're all polished up and nicely turned out! What's the occasion?"

Curran did a slow, deep blush. "No occasion. I just thought I . . ."

He didn't finish his sentence, because Claire had stepped up to the bar. She was dressed in a soft, blue tank top and matching skirt. Tied over her shoulders was a deep, ocean-blue sweater. Her hair was up away from her face, making her eyes seem larger and darker. The pearl studs in her ears were the only jewelry she wore, their pale luminescence accenting the creamy olive tone of her skin. She was what is commonly referred to as "drop-dead beautiful." Curran couldn't speak; he just stared at her.

"Hello, gentlemen," she said, as she stood back, waiting to be invited closer.

Hawkins was the first to recover. He hopped off his stool and grinned broadly. "Well, hello! Let's see, it was Dulles Airport, right?"

Claire raised an eyebrow. "And you, you're involved with an escort service, right?"

Hawkins began to piece the picture together. He slapped Curran on the back. "The airport, RIGHT! Good work, boss! I'm proud of you."

Curran gave him a get-lost look, then turned back to Claire. "Claire Verens, Dale Hawkins. She's down here for business."

As they shook hands, Hawkins looked at her inquisitively. "And what might that business be?"

"Middle East terrorism," Curran said, beginning to burn as Hawkins continued to hold Claire's hand.

Claire looked up coolly at Hawkins. "If you don't turn loose my hand, I'm going to have to charge you rent."

Hawkins pretended embarrassment. "Oh, excuse me," he said, relinquishing his hold. "But how does a girl—I mean, a woman—become an expert in terrorism?"

Curran grabbed her arm and began to steer her away from the bar. "I'm starved! How about you?" he asked, ignoring Hawkins.

"Gosh, boss, I feel like I haven't eaten for days," Hawkins answered, as if the question had been directed to him.

"I wasn't speaking to you." Curran cut his eyes, warning Hawkins away.

Hawkins looked from Curran to Claire, then back. He quickly assumed a pitiful look. "Sorry. I was just about to head down to Phil's. They have a special for single, very lonely diners. Nice to see you again." He turned and began to walk away sadly, his shoulders slumped as he headed toward the door.

Claire laughed and nudged Curran. "He's such a bad actor." She called out to Hawkins, who was barely moving, "Come on, you can eat with us."

Hawkins whirled around and started toward them. Curran blanched as Claire smiled teasingly at him.

"Well," said Hawkins as he hurried up to them, "I really shouldn't."

"You're right, Hawk," Curran said quickly, cutting him off. "You really shouldn't."

"Oh, but then again"—he smiled maliciously at Curran—"maybe I should."

Claire laughed again as Curran shot daggers at Hawkins, who smiled back at him.

"Do you like crab?" Hawkins asked, taking control and guiding Claire toward the door. "Because if you do, I know where they serve the best crab in the bay. You know the place, boss—Carol's House of Crab. In fact, we'll go in my car. . . . You drive."

"Damn you, Hawk!" Curran whispered to him as they passed through the door. Hawkins pretended not to hear and continued to keep up a steady, inane banter all the way to the restaurant. Claire was amused, laughing occasionally at some of Hawkins's remarks. A storm brewed on the other side of the bay, and streaks of lightning flashed and danced on the far shore.

This is not going well, Curran thought as they pulled into the restaurant's parking lot. Time was running out on them.

Later, slamming a wooden mallet down on a large red crab, Hawkins sent bits of shell and cartilage flying everywhere. A claw flipped into the air and landed on a woman sitting across from them. She jumped as it landed, then snatched it out of her lap and turned to see where it had come from.

Hawkins mouthed "I'm sorry!" as Claire struggled not to laugh out loud.

Curran was pissed, but he was trying not to show it. The pitcher of beer sitting in front of them was almost empty.

Carol's House of Crab was out on one of the jetties. Sailboats and yachts were moored along the walkway, and the swaying lights from the piers twinkled off the water.

The restaurant was a typical dock place—the kind that tourists read about but can never find. Only the natives ate there, and they didn't encourage outsiders, for fear the prices would go up. Long formica tables lined the walls. Each patron got a piece of butcher paper to eat from as their order of steaming Chesapeake Bay crab was delivered. The seating was either on benches or gray metal auditorium-style chairs, the kind that could be folded up and stacked. Large drains were sunk in the concrete floors about every fifteen feet, so that when the place closed at night, the help could just sweep up, then turn on the hoses and wash the place down.

Harried waitresses bustled from table to table, a little on the crabby side themselves. What the place lacked in hospitality, it made up for in good food.

Along with steamed crab and beer, they served a crisp mixed salad and homemade bread. There was a line of people waiting to get in, and the line seldom thinned out from opening time to closing.

"You missed this piece!" Hawkins grabbed Claire's arm and ate a large chunk of crabmeat that had landed on her elbow from his last smashing blow. Claire laughed and pushed him away. Curran sat at the table seething, tossing a salt shaker from one hand to the other.

Wiping bits of crab from his shirt, Hawkins stood. "Please excuse me. . . . Gotta answer a call from nature. Don't let Curran take you away while I'm gone." He smiled as he turned and walked to the back of the restaurant.

"Take your time," Curran called after him.

"Don't you like him?" Claire asked, watching as Hawkins disappeared down a hallway marked "Telephone—Restrooms."

"More some days than others. Not much tonight."

"Well, he's gone now. What did you want to ask me?" Claire wiped her hands with a napkin and reached for her beer.

"I'd like to know a little more about Ben Shaheed. Where he's headquartered. Where he might hole up if he were in trouble."

"Is he in trouble?" Claire asked, gazing at Curran over the top of her beer mug.

"He's a terrorist. Terrorists are all in trouble."

"Because the SEALs are after them?"

"Do you know where he is?" Curran stared at her.

Claire placed the mug back on the table. "Not yet, Curran. You're moving too fast. I want some answers to some of my questions, too. Why are you looking for him? . . . It's more than curiosity with you. . . . It's personal, isn't it?"

"This isn't the place to talk about this. It isn't even the place I wanted to go. When Hawkins gets back, we'll get rid of him and I'll try to explain—as much as I can, that is." Curran crumbled his napkin and placed it on the table.

Hawkins dropped a coin in the telephone slot and punched in seven numbers on the face of the pay phone. There were two quick rings; then a voice answered on the other end.

"Yes, Message Center?" Hawkins answered, disguising his voice. "This is Captain Dunne."

As he walked back to the table, Hawkins noticed that Curran and Claire were not talking. She was gazing disinterestedly at the other diners, while Curran tossed the salt shaker from one hand to another.

Sitting down, Hawkins looked past Claire at Curran and said, "Hey, Curran, you better loosen up. Why so glum?" He flashed his friendliest smile as Curran looked up at him, disgusted.

Claire turned to Curran. "How long have you been friends?" she asked as she slapped at Hawkins, who was trying to lick a drop of butter off her arm.

"Too long," Curran said, not at all amused by Hawkins's antics.

"Boss, that's cold!" Hawkins feigned a hurt look. "Why, he's my idol! Some day I want to be just like him," he said, directing all of his attention at Claire.

115

"That man," Curran said, rapidly beginning to lose patience with Hawkins, "is a pathological liar."

Claire sensed the tension, though she didn't understand exactly where it was coming from. "Okay, okay. A question: Why did you both decide to become SEALs?"

First to answer, Hawkins affected deep concentration. "Uh, I don't exactly remember. But there was something very important that made me do it. Oh YES, it was the women! SEALs always had the finest-looking women! It was like joining the best frat on campus."

Claire shook her head. "My, but that is a profound and meaningful reason. What about you, Curran?"

Continuing to toss the salt shaker back and forth, Curran looked up at her. "Do you think this atmosphere of frivolity could stand a serious answer?" he asked, wishing deeply that Hawkins would disappear.

"It was a serious question," Claire answered.

He took a deep breath. "I was studying oceanography at San Diego State and got to know a couple of SEALs," he said, putting the shaker down on the table. "The idea of combining a love of the ocean with my perhaps outdated notion of serving my country appealed to me."

She looked at him, and they were both silent. Hawkins noticed and decided to break it up. "Hey, don't you want to hear my serious answer?"

"No," Claire said, continuing to stare at Curran.

"Okay." Hawkins plowed on undaunted, stuffing his face with crabmeat: "Ask me another question."

Claire smiled at Curran, who looked skyward in desperation.

"Do you share Lieutenant Curran's fascination with the Mideast, Hawkins?" she asked.

"You mean Lebanon? Nah," he said, wiping his mouth with a paper napkin.

"You haven't been there, I take it?"

Hawkins curled his lip as though he smelled something disgusting. "Who in their right mind would go there? Rags knocking each other off like its the national pastime?"

Claire's smile dropped "*Rags?*" She looked at Hawkins for an explanation.

Hawkins now had a large crab claw in his hand and was using it to gesture with. "The ragheads. You know, A-rabs."

A dark look clouded her face as Claire's entire body tensed.

Hawkins, paying no attention, continued to rave on, swinging the crab claw around wildly. "I think they're all half nuts. As far as I'm concerned, those fanatics can keep on blowing each other's head off till they're all wiped out. Maybe then we might have a little peace."

Using a piece of bread, he shoveled up some crab-meat he'd dropped on the table. He hadn't looked up the entire time he'd been ranting. As he trapped the meat on the bread crust, he flipped his head up and tossed it into his mouth. He noticed, looking over, that Claire's face was crimson.

Outside, the thunder heard earlier sounded nearer. The storm rolled in across the bay.

Hawkins looked down the table to Curran, who

117

was giving him shut-up signals, which he ignored. "Did I say something wrong?" he asked.

Claire's voice came out thin and reedy. "I happen to be half 'RAG' myself. My mother was Lebanese. I was born in Beirut and spent the first twelve years of my life there." She was visibly shaking.

Hawkins recovered with incredible speed. "I knew THAT! I knew that, I was just putting you on! I mean, Lebanese women are the most beautiful women in the world. Why, I knew—the moment I saw you—that you were—"

"Can the bullshit, Hawkins," Curran cut in.

"And another thing," Claire continued, "I'm going to try to enlighten your narrow, racist, xenophobic, and uninformed mind. Islam doesn't preach terrorism. It is one of the most tolerant religions, built on equality and justice. But there's not much of either in the Middle East. The real war going on in Beirut isn't religious. It's a battle to escape poverty and despair, a battle to gain some small amount of dignity." There were tears of anger in the corners of her eyes, but she quickly dabbed them away with a napkin.

A silence fell over the table, as neither man knew what to say. The silence was ended abruptly as a loud beeping sound issued from Curran's pager. He pulled it out and read the digital readout. "Damn! Captain Dunne wants me at headquarters!"

"TOO bad!" said Hawkins innocently.

A loud clap of thunder sounded through the open patio, followed by a blinding flash of lightning. The skies that had been threatening before now opened, and the rain came pouring down.

Curran pulled some money from his pocket and

handed it to Claire. "I'm sorry. I have to leave. This should cover dinner and cab fare back to your car. You can drive me over, Hawkins."

Claire shoved the money back at Curran. "I can take care of it," she said, rising from her chair.

Hawkins grabbed the bills and jumped up from his chair. "A better solution: . . . You pay for the dinner, Curran, and I'll give Claire a ride to her car. You take a cab." He put his hand on Claire's shoulder and guided her away from the table.

Stunned, Curran watched as Hawkins threw the money down on the counter and rushed out the door with Claire to the car. He could hear the GTO pulling away from the restaurant as he went to use a pay phone.

Claire had both hands on the dashboard, bracing herself, as Hawkins roared through the marina. "You are a maniac! Slow this damned thing down!"

"I don't know if I can! You see, the car has a mind of its own," Hawkins answered, beginning to slow down.

"If it does, then it's the only intelligent life form in here!" She released her grip on the dash and dug both hands into the sides of her seat.

"I wanted to tell you a little about myself, now that I know a lot about you." He smiled his most charming smile as he began to operate within the legal speed limit.

"I think I know all I want to about you. Take me to my car, please." Claire was still not calm, but she was somewhat less frightened now that the lightposts were becoming less of a blur by the side of the road.

"We're on our way. Anyway, I grew up in the wet-back section of Fresno," he said, beginning his life story as he slowed for a red light.

Claire turned and looked at him. "I think they're called Mexicans."

Hawkins slammed his palm against his forehead. "Are you going to actually make me think before I talk?"

"Try it. It will be a totally new experience for you."

Making a turn at the next light, Hawkins guided the car down to the boardwalk and came to a stop on a sandy strip of beach.

"So, where was I?" He began to search through a box of cassettes. "Oh . . . anyway, my mom taught school and my dad, when he did work, supervised fruit pickers. He used to drive around in a golf cart. A Jap . . . *enese*"—he flashed a quick grin—"mine blew both his feet off, so he couldn't get around too good. He thinks I'm nuts for being a fulltime frog-man." He slipped a cassette into the slot in the dash, and the music of Steve Windwood filled the car.

Claire looked at him in disbelief. "What are you doing? Why are we stopped?"

Ignoring her questions, Hawkins tapped out the rhythm on the steering wheel. "This stuff is great, isn't it? Have you got a favorite? . . . I might have it here in my repertoire."

"Yeah," Claire answered. "Do you know 'Turn This Car Around and Take Me to My Car'?"

He laughed. "It's great out here. Look, the rain has stopped. I like to—"

"See ya!" Claire cut in, as she opened the door and stepped out onto the sand.

Hawkins jumped out of the car and ran around to the other side, cutting her off as she headed toward the boardwalk. "Hey! I'll take you back. But what's your hurry? We got an ocean with lots of romantic surf pounding. We got two people strongly attracted to each other—"

"TWO?" Claire interrupted, scowling at him.

"Well, one outta two ain't bad." Hawkins beamed a boyish grin.

"Look, you're an amusing guy and you're kind of attractive—"

"*Kind* of attractive?"

"To a certain type, maybe. But I'm not remotely interested. So, if you don't mind, please take me back to my car."

Hawkins hung his head and opened the passenger side for her, then walked around and meekly slid in next to her. He started the engine and began to drive up through the undergrowth to the street.

"I guess this means that you're not going to sleep with me tonight," Hawkins said softly. He looked over at Claire, his face the picture of innocence.

She turned to face him, prepared to give him the ass-chewing of his life, then began to laugh.

"You are the most ridiculous person I have ever met!" They drove back to her car and parted in the parking lot. Claire was still laughing, but she felt safer as soon as she locked her doors.

12

The next morning, Hawkins reported to SEAL headquarters, slipped into his black fatigues, and entered a dark room. As he walked in, a single spotlight snapped on over him. He pulled his pistol from his shoulder holster and held it in front of his chest, both arms bent at the elbow, as he stared out into the dark. A screen lit up directly in front of him, then another flashed on his left and another to his right.

Curran, also in black fatigues, stood next to the front screen, arms folded, staring at Hawkins. An image flickered to life on the screens. The footage being shown was an everyday scene in the main lobby of the Vienna airport. There were travelers carrying luggage, walking back and forth, jostling for positions in line at the ticket counters. On the far-left screen, ten masked gunmen burst into view, firing into the crowd.

Hawkins's arms shot out in front of him. Braced, he fired in short, two-shot bursts at the images, sending pieces of the screen whipping into the darkness. He spun with the pistol, firing first to the left, then right, then center and back again, responding to the images that flashed before him.

A terrorist on the screen grabbed a woman by the hair, about to put his gun to her head. Hawkins fired, dropping the gunman. A young, panic-stricken man plunged forward, waving a cane. Hawkins swung his pistol up past the man and fired at the terrorist behind him, hitting the gunman with both shots.

Pandemonium broke out as two terrorists cut loose with AK47s into the crowd. Terrified people began to run, scattering in all directions and obscuring the gunmen momentarily. Curran watched as Hawkins grappled with the view, then fired two more bursts, finding his way through the chaos to his targets.

The images on the screen began to fade. Hawkins pulled the gun back to his chest, paused for a moment, then returned the gun to its holster. The lights came on in the room as the screens went dark. The room was actually a large projection room; the white paper hanging from the walls was riddled with bullet holes.

Hawkins nodded to Curran as he stepped up next to him.

"Run it back," Curran called up to the projectionist.

The lights went down and the screens again began to flicker with life. The scene was replayed, only this time, as the terrorists were shot, the images would freeze, revealing the exact position of each of Hawkins's bullets.

"Hold it!" Curran called out to the man running the film. The images stopped on the screen in mid-action. "Okay," Curran ordered, "run it back." The film moved slowly in reverse. "Stop there." Curran had found the spot he was looking for. Hawkins watched, a puzzled look on his face.

"There." Curran moved to the screen. "You dropped a shot." The frozen image on the screen indicated that one of Hawkins's shots had been dead center and the other had missed the target by no more than an inch. Hawkins moved over closer to the screen, examined the missed shot, then looked up at Curran.

"So I missed one," he said indignantly. "Big fuckin' deal."

Curran continued looking at the screen, his back to Hawkins as he spoke. "There's no such thing in our business. You either score or you're dead. You don't qualify."

Hawkins grabbed Curran's shoulder and yanked him around, facing him. "What? Because of one lousy dropped shot?" He was enraged. "Since when does one dropped shot disqualify?"

Curran called up to the projectionist, "Turn it off and leave us for five minutes."

"Aye, sir," came the response from the overhead chamber as the lights again flicked on.

There was no hint of hostility on Curran's face, just quiet resolve. "In answer to your question, Hawkins, since now."

"I just don't believe I'm hearing this!" Hawkins threw his arms up and began to pace aggressively in front of the screens. He stopped and whirled around to face Curran. "Wait. . . . I get it! This isn't about a dropped shot at all! This is about last night." He pointed a finger in Curran's face. "You're pissed at me because I got in the way of your heavy romance!"

Pushing the hand out of his face, Curran answered, slowly and deliberately, "No, Hawk . . . you're not even remotely close."

"Bullshit I'm not!" Hawkins pushed his hands in his pockets and turned around, facing the wall.

Curran started toward the door, then stopped. "You know, Hawk, just once, when you're encountering a female, why don't you try thinking with your head and not your cock?"

"All's fair in love and war. . . ."

Curran clenched his jaw. "Everything's a fucking game to you! That woman could have information helpful in locating the Stingers."

Hawkins spun around and faced him, a look of disbelief on his face. "Oh, yeah, and like the CIA has somehow overlooked her, right? What are you, a goddamn spook now, Curran? Jesus Christ, who do you think you are! . . . James Bond?"

Curran explained, "I was trying to convince her to share that information when you came along and blew the evening with one of your wacko performances."

"I guess you expect me to buy that crock?" said Hawkins, feeling a little less sure of himself than before. He jutted out his chin. "I suppose it's just a coincidence that she's gorgeous?"

Choosing to ignore this remark, Curran motioned to the screen. "Let's set it up. You can do it again."

Hawkins brusquely handed the gun to Curran. "Here, you do it again! By the way, we fucked all night, like two crazed snakes in a barrel!" He pushed past Curran and slammed the door behind him.

13

Claire walked briskly down the road fronting the airfield. She wore jeans and a sweatshirt and carried a briefcase in her left hand. Row after row of F-16s, F-4 Phantoms, and F-18s sat on the tarmac, the sunlight bouncing off their slick metal skins.

Hawkins's red GTO pulled up a yard or two behind her on the road. He yelled out to her over the windshield, "Need a lift?"

Startled, Claire turned around. She shook her head. "You'd have to be one silver-tongued devil to get me back in that thing . . . and you're not!" She continued walking as Hawkins glided along beside her.

"You really need to get to know me better! I'm a pretty incredible guy."

Claire continued to walk, looking out at the planes as she ignored the man creeping alongside her in the convertible. "I'm happy for you."

Hawkins laid his head on his arm and steered the car slowly beside her. "I read your book last night."

Without slowing down or even looking at him, Claire answered, "Oh, sure you did. What was the title?"

"The cover had been removed and run through the shredder. Security, you know." He grinned as she glanced over at him, then looked back at the hangars. "Okay, I didn't read it, but I read the synopsis. Good stuff!"

"Hah!" She quickened her pace. "You'll never know how much I appreciate a literary review from you!"

Hawkins straightened up in the seat, pulling his arm back into the car. "Say, some buddies of mine are having a cookout over on their cruiser tonight, and if you're not busy . . ."

Claire came to an abrupt stop and turned around to face him. "Does the word *no* have any meaning at all to you?"

He shook his head and smiled. "Very little."

She threw her head back and looked up into the sky, then continued walking. Hawkins pulled up beside her again, looking her over from her ankles to her head. "Well," he said, slowly, as if in thought, "maybe you're not my type after all. I generally like 'em a little blonder, younger, and a lot dumber."

Claire smiled. "Figures." The road widened as it crossed the street where the SEAL headquarters was located. She started to cross the street, but Hawkins pulled in front of her, blocking her way.

"I've got the perfect guy for you." He hung his arm over the side of the car and slapped a rhythmic beat against the door. "Similar interests, personalities, taste in clothes. Come to think of it, I'm pretty sure he would go for a half-Lebanese journalist with a Harvard degree. You know who I'm talking about?" He grinned, watching her.

"Get out of my life, Mr. Hawkins!" Claire thumped her briefcase on the hood of the GTO.

"Dane ... You know him—great with guns, big guy, never talks ... Perfect for you, just perfect!" Hawkins put the car in gear and blasted past her, laughing hysterically.

Claire groaned and watched him speed away. She stepped up on the curb and walked up to the SEAL headquarters.

A young seaman was sitting at the desk in front as Claire walked in. He rose from his chair and waited until she got to the desk.

"Yes, ma'am, what can I do for you?" he asked, appraising the woman standing in front of him.

"Could you check and see if Lieutenant Curran is in? Tell him Claire Verens is here." She pulled her briefcase up onto the desk, removed a card, and handed it to him.

"Yes, ma'am, he's here. I'll go tell him you're waiting. Won't you have a seat please." He motioned to some chairs along the wall. As Claire sat down, the young man disappeared down a hallway.

Several Navy enlisted men and officers came through the doors, all of them wearing tridents, the SEAL insignia, on their uniforms. Claire recognized a few of the SEALs she had seen the day before in the training sessions. One of them, the medic called Leary, waved at her as he walked by. After a few minutes, Curran came hurrying down the corridor with the seaman, who was trying, without success, to match his strides. Curran was still in the black fatigues he had worn in the target room.

"Hello—I didn't expect to see you," he said, greeting her.

"I've come to keep my end of the bargain. I thought about some of the things you said yesterday, about not having any more time. So let's stop wasting it. Do you have some place we can talk?" She had never seen that uniform before. The black fatigues suited him, looking as natural on him as skin on bone. He seemed more relaxed, she thought, because he was in his own atmosphere, on his hallowed turf.

"My office," he said, indicating that it was back down the corridor that he had emerged from.

"Let's go." She let him lead the way down the hall. As Curran opened the door to the office, Hawkins stepped out of the office across the hall.

"Claire!" he said, affecting an air of familiarity. "Why, my dear, I had no idea you were headed this way."

This time she warned him off. "Look, Lieutenant Curran asked me to help him with this terrorist material. I've come to do that—only that—then I'm out of here. Save your charm for someone blonder and dumber."

His attitude and manner changed suddenly. "I'd like to sit in if it's permissible, boss. I'll keep my mouth shut."

Curran looked at Hawkins. There had been a change since their session that morning—nothing big, but the Hawk seemed quieter. "See that you do, and you're welcome to join us."

Curran waited until Claire and Hawkins had entered the room, then he stepped in and closed the door. They sat down at a small table Curran hurriedly cleared of papers.

"Excuse me," Curran asked as she sat down, "would you like something to drink? I can send for it."

"No, I'm fine," Claire replied. "Let's get started."

She pulled a folder containing papers and photographs from her briefcase and placed it in front of her. Curran reached out, but she put her hand on it, pulling it back before he could pick it up. "The Al Shuhada faction we're concerned with is centered mainly in the Beqaa Valley. It's headed by this man."

The black-and-white photo she held in her hand was a picture of the stranger they had seen at the port.

Hawkins stared in wonder. "It's our buddy, Popeye the Sailorman."

"Who?" Claire asked.

Curran waved off the question. "Never mind, go on."

Claire laid the picture in the center of the table as she spoke. "His name is Kahlil Hussein Musawi, but he calls himself Ben Shaheed. That means 'son of the martyr.' He's thirty-seven years old, born in Beirut, attended the American university there, lived for five years in New York, where he was a student at Columbia, as well as a Broadway-theater critic for the Arab journals. Came home with an unaccountable, almost pathological hatred for the United States."

"Probably because he couldn't get laid." Hawkins laughed.

Curran slid his chair back. "Hawkins, you promised."

Hawkins put his hand over his mouth. "Excuse me. Go on."

She pulled out another black-and-white photo and laid it down next to Shaheed's. The man in this photograph was large and corpulent, with a close-trimmed beard and a hook nose. He was wearing enough jewelry to make Elizabeth Taylor swoon.

"This one," she said, pointing to the picture, "is Amal Fahladi. He's the money man. It's believed that all the funding for the Al Shuhada flows through him." She started to pull another photo out.

"Where is he located?" Curran asked, quickly scribbling down some notes.

Claire hesitated for a moment. "He has a beach-front villa in Sidon. Now, this one—"

"Hold it a minute," interrupted Hawkins. "I have a question." He turned to Curran. "Wouldn't this money man know where the missiles are?"

Curran's face paled. "Shut up!"

"Missiles? No, please go on. I want to hear about the missiles." Claire sat up on the edge of her chair and leaned forward.

Taking a deep breath, Curran looked over at Hawkins and shook his head. "Okay, we have reason to believe that Ben Shaheed has a number of missiles, and we want them."

"Humm, what kind of missiles and how many?" she asked, not about to be put off now.

"Look, I'm telling you this—and I'm hoping that you'll treat 'in the strictest confidentiality' with the same reverence as you treat 'protection of sources.' . . . Stingers, he's got Stingers. . . . We saw three crates of them." Curran fumbled with the pictures on the table.

She whistled. "Stingers! I guess you are desperate. Where did you see them and when?"

Curran looked up at her, and his face became blank. "That, Ms. Verens, is not something we can discuss. I've already said more than I should have. Please, let's go on."

Claire started to protest, then stopped. "Okay. You're right, Hawkins. Amal Fahladi would know where the missiles are."

"Boss!" Hawkins's eyes began to glow brightly. "This is simple! We snatch him and make him talk."

Before Curran could answer, Claire began to shake her head. "There's that Western mind at work!" she said, her voice getting that flinty edge to it again. "Remember, these are religious zealots. There is no way you could make them talk."

Hawkins picked up a pen from the table and began to push steadily on the point retractor, making a series of clicking noises. He seemed deep in thought. "Hey!" he said at last. "What if we did an imitation of the Russians?"

Claire turned to Curran, watching his guarded expression, as Hawkins began to speak excitedly. "Don't you remember when those three Russian diplomats were taken hostage? The Russians snatched the families of the kidnapers. Those diplomats were home for dinner!"

"There's a good reason for that. Everything in the Middle East revolves around the family." Claire lowered her eyes and looked at the tiny silver band around her wrist. "There are ties . . . blood ties."

133

"Tell me about Fahladi's family tree." Curran did not look at her as he spoke. He seemed to be studying what he had written on the paper.

Claire pushed back away from the table. "Is that why you wanted to talk to me? . . . To make me part of some illegal kidnaping operation?"

Curran's head snapped up, his eyes again smoldering with intensity. "Just asking a question."

She stood and picked up the photos, putting them back into the folder. As she opened her briefcase to put the folder inside, she looked over at Curran, her anger beginning to show. "Don't you think, Lieutenant Curran, that adopting the tactics of the terrorists makes one a terrorist himself?" She slammed the briefcase and stood up with it in her hand, waiting for Curran to answer.

Hawkins and Curran stood up, looking at her.

"Not necessarily, Ms. Verens," said Curran, "but apparently you do."

She turned and walked to the door, pausing for a minute before she opened it. "Oh, I do indeed." She reached for the doorknob and pulled it open. "Goodbye," she said, as she closed the door behind her.

Hawkins looked over at Curran, who was still staring at the door. "Boss, nothing happened last night. I just wanted you to know that."

Curran sighed and looked down at his desk. "I know that, Hawkins." He picked up the notes and crammed them into his pocket. "You're good, but you're not that good."

"And I'm sorry—about last night, I mean."

Curran reached over and lightly clipped his shoulder. "No problem, Hawk. Claire Verens and I see things . . . peculiarly . . . sometimes too much alike

134

and, then again, not alike at all. Want to have a go at the targets again?" Curran raised his eyebrows, challenging Hawkins.

"You bet your ass, boss. Let's do it to it."

Hawkins and Curran left the room together and walked down to the screen room. In the second round, Hawkins never dropped a shot.

After they had finished, Curran left for Langley, carrying the notes he had made during Claire's short briefing.

14

It was midafternoon in Madrid. The cool winds from the north blew into the city, signaling the end of fall. It had rained earlier but stopped at noon. The air was damp and heavy with humidity.

The old rooftop was wavy, the result of long years of heavy use and poor repairs. Small puddles of water stood in the low spots and reflected the clouds above like tiny pieces of a broken mirror.

A group of children played on the vacant lot three stories below, the sound of their shouts and cries carried on the wind and mixed with the cacophony of the car horns and heavy traffic on the tiny streets. Madrid was a large, beautiful city, but some of the most heavily used streets had been built by the Romans on their way to Africa.

Two men, carrying a heavy metal case, emerged from a stairwell and walked onto the wavy roof. They set the case down, opened it, and removed a long, thin weapon. They screwed a small cylinder onto the weapon and waited.

Both men were dressed in Western suits, but their coloring indicated that they were Middle Easterners. Both men had black, curly beards, and they both had a fiery, unnerving look in their eyes.

They exchanged few words as they worked on the weapon. One of the men glanced down at his watch and nodded to the other, who lifted the missile-launcher to his shoulder and flipped up the sight bar. Over the rooftops, a private jet appeared in the missile's sight. The man holding the launcher fired, and the missile exploded off his shoulder.

The Stinger's rocket motor ignited, and the five-foot missile streaked off after the jet, leaving a thin white plume of smoke behind it. It flew off to one side a bit, causing the gunner to mutter curses, but then it turned and streaked toward the jet, slamming into it. The jet exploded in a huge orange fireball. Pieces of the jet fell, trailing wisps of smoke.

On the roof, the gunner stood transfixed. His companion whooped and shouted, "Allahu Akbar!"

As the pieces of the doomed jet fell, the two men unlatched the spent missile tube and discarded it, placing the gripstock unit in a nylon shoulder bag. They quickly ran down the stairs and signaled to a waiting BMW. Ten seconds later, they disappeared into the swirling Madrid traffic.

15

Curran and his team sat at a table in Captain Dunne's office, their eyes glued to a television monitor. An anchorman was speaking, while footage of rescue-team workers, sifting through smoking wreckage on a hilltop, flashed across the screen. "To recap our lead story: A private jet, leaving Madrid for London, was shot down early this morning by what experts believe to have been a missile, fired from an undetermined location."

Dunne sat in his chair, rubbing his big hands together. "That's just a taste of what's at stake here," he said.

Claire was in the bedroom of her apartment, lying across the bed, listening to the same report. "All twelve aboard, including an Algerian negotiating committee, are presumed dead. There are unconfirmed reports that the weapon which downed the plane was an American-built Stinger missile."

Claire pulled herself upright and sat on the side

of the bed. Her face was etched with the horror and sadness she felt. "So far," the anchorman continued, "four Middle East terrorist groups have claimed credit." Claire reached over and turned off the set. She touched the little silver bracelet, then buried her face in her hands, sobbing uncontrollably.

Later, she rose from the bed and went into the bathroom to take a long, hot shower. When she emerged from the shower stall, she wrapped her hair in a towel, then wrapped another towel around her slender body. Steam covered the mirror over her make-up counter, so she bent down and turned on her hair-dryer.

Moving the blower back and forth, she cleared the mirror, then sat down and began to rub the towel through her hair. The intercom buzzer sounded, startling her. She grabbed her robe from a hook behind the door and hurriedly pulled it on as she ran through the kitchen to the master intercom in the living room. She tapped the switch. "Yes?"

"Claire . . . it's James Curran. May I come up?"

"Oh, I . . . well . . . okay, come on up." She pushed the buzzer and unlocked the entry.

Curran walked up the stairs to the landing and tapped on the door. "It's open!" Claire called out from inside.

He opened the door and walked into her living room.

"I'll be out in a minute. Make yourself comfortable."

He could have, too. The room wasn't very large, but she had furnished it well. An oversized beige leather couch was centered opposite a fireplace, and a large flokati rug was spread out over the hardwood floors. There were several pillows in varying shades of blue and turquoise, scattered around on the fluffy, sheep's-wool rug.

A glass shelving unit stood in the entry hall. Curran looked at the things neatly arranged on each tier.

There were many pictures on the shelves. Some of them were of a woman who looked very much like Claire but older. Others were group shots, obviously of family gatherings, with grandparents, parents, and lots of children sitting at the feet of the elders. The people in the pictures were all smiling and happy. In the background of one of the pictures was a mosque. Curran looked more closely at the picture.

All the pictures had been taken somewhere in the Middle East part of the world. Probably Beirut, Curran thought to himself. But maybe not; it looked too good to be Beirut.

The Beirut he remembered wasn't beautiful. It was like a bad nightmare, a city of ruins and fires, filth and poverty, of skinny dogs and skinnier children. He remembered the screams of the dying and the flat broken sobs of women, mourning their losses.

He was still standing there, looking at the pictures, when Claire walked into the room. She stepped up next to him and looked at the photograph in his hand. He was holding one of the big group shots. Her hair was damp, falling heavily around her head, and she smelled of roses and cinnamon.

She reached over and took the picture from his hands. "That was taken the year before I left Beirut.

See"—she pointed to a thin young girl in pony-tails—"that's me. It was my grandmother's birth-day. She was seventy-five on that day." She smiled as she looked at the photo, then placed it back on the shelf.

"Where does she live today? Paris?" Curran asked, still looking at the pictures.

"She doesn't live today. None of the people in those pictures are alive, except me." She turned and walked away from him and sat down on the couch. "They either died in the shellings or they died of broken hearts. People still die of that, you know. We call it 'losing the will to live,' but it's all the same."

Curran's eyes widened as she spoke, and he stared at her lost family. All the faces smiling out of those frames had died. It was almost impossible to believe that an entire family had been wiped off the face of the earth.

"God, Claire. You never mentioned . . . you never said anything . . . " He struggled for words as he turned around to face her.

"That was then, this is now. I'm alive, I have my work. I don't like to talk about that." She looked across the room at the man standing there. "I know why you're here. It's about the jet that was shot down in Madrid. It doesn't change anything."

"What are you talking about?" He stepped around the couch and sat down next to her.

"You're here to convince me that the plane that was shot down was just the first of many. And if I don't help you recover the other missiles, there might be blood on my hands. Isn't that right?"

Curran cleared his throat. "I wouldn't have said

it that way." She was beautiful, sitting there in a T-shirt and jeans, her hair still damp. Her face was clean, with no make-up, revealing the true beauty of her features. Straightforward and honest; everything about her was right. Curran realized with a jolt why he was so uneasy around her.

"I'm a journalist," she said, standing up and walking over to the window. "I don't create the news, I report it."

"There must be certain times when you know you can make a difference." Curran stood up and followed her.

"Oh, please, Curran. My principles don't change according to the weather." Her voice was low and soft, as if she were pleading with him to understand, while knowing that he couldn't.

Curran looked from her face out onto the gardens below. He was frantically searching for some way they could compromise. "This is a crisis," he said. "Lives are at stake."

She sighed and wiped at her eyes. "Lebanon has been in a crisis for thirteen years. And lives have always been at stake."

"So we do nothing?" he asked.

"You believe you're the good guys—the SEALs—and they're the bad guys—the terrorists. Well, they believe just the opposite. For the people of Lebanon, it doesn't matter who's right."

Curran hesitated, then put his arm around her, pulling her near him. He had his thumb under her chin and turned her face up to his. "I believe it should matter." They stood for a long time, holding on to their moment of closeness. Then Claire stepped back, away from him.

"Do you think it mattered to my family and friends in Beirut whether the shells that killed them came from Christian, Muslim, or Israeli guns?" she asked.

"I believe what we're doing will help stop it all." Curran held his hand out to her.

She stared down at his hand. "I believe *YOU* do, but all you're really doing is perpetuating the madness, the endless cycle of terrorism. Victims becoming victimizers, then they trade roles . . . back and forth . . . on and on. I hope some day, someone will find a way to stop it." She reached out and placed her hand in his.

Curran looked down at the long slender fingers that curled around his and the little silver bangle around her wrists. It was almost perfect, but as she turned her hand, he noticed that one side of the band was malformed, as if it had melted. "Just turn the other cheek?" Curran asked.

She pulled her hand back slowly. "Can you give me your word that the SEALs will not be kidnaping hostages to extort information?"

He looked at her sadly; the compromise had not been reached. "You know I can't do that."

Claire took a deep breath. A tear rolled down her cheek as she shook her head. "Then I'm sorry. Our deal is off. I can't give you any more information." She walked to the door. "Good-bye, Curran."

"That bracelet . . . where did you get it?"

"My parent's home in Beirut was shelled—not on purpose; it was just in the way. When the fires stopped, they went in to clear the wreckage and to look for my mother. They only thing that they could save was this bracelet. My father gave it to her on their wedding day. She never took it off. It's all that I have left."

"I'm sorry, Claire. I hoped . . . we came . . . Goodbye." He stared at her for a moment, then walked past her, out the door and onto the landing, closing the door behind him. He felt numb as he walked down the stairs. When he reached the bottom, he stood there in the breezeway. He started to turn around and go back up the steps but realized that he couldn't. There was a broad gulf between them, and he wasn't sure that understanding and caring could bridge the gap. He would still be what he was, and she would never change the way she felt.

Walking out to his jeep, he suddenly felt cold and alone, more alone than he'd ever felt before. He climbed into the jeep and decided to take the long route back to headquarters, out over the Chesapeake Bridge.

He wasn't sure why he had gone to Claire's in the first place. It had been a bad move—one of his worst. All the way to his office, he could smell roses and cinnamon.

16

Stinson's office looked the same as it had the last time Curran and Dunne had been there. Curran checked the chair he'd sat in, to see if any burnt remnant of his ass remained there. James Elmore greeted them with an inquisitive look and a nod, while Eliot West suppressed a yawn and drummed his fingers on the tabletop. Behind the big cluttered desk, Stinson was doing his routine pacing of the area, pausing for a moment to greet them, then resuming the nervous activity. "Good to see you," he said as they took their places at the table. "I understand you've come up with a plan, Lieutenant Curran. Please, share it with us."

Curran stood up and opened his folder. He held up a photo of the Arab money man. "This is Amal Fahladi. He's the guy who knows where the missiles are. He wouldn't talk even if we could get to him." He laid the photo down on the table and pulled another from the folder. "This man," he said, holding up the photo so everyone could see, "is

Amal's brother, Assad, who doesn't know where the missiles are but who we can get to."

The two photos made their way around the table. West stopped drumming on the table and and picked up the picture of Amal Fahladi. "Where did you get this?" he asked, thumping the photograph with his forefinger.

"Your office," Dunne answered, smiling. "Thanks for sharing it with us."

"Here's where he lives," Curran continued, holding up an aerial photograph. "It's Sidon, a city just south of Beirut. Notice"—he pointed to the photo—"it's three city blocks from the shoreline. A high-altitude-low-opening—or HALO—drop, snatch and grab, and we've got him."

Elmore leaned back in his chair, rubbing the stubble on his chin. He stretched an arm forward and picked up the aerial photo, waving it in front of him. "What does all this mean, Lieutenant?"

Curran looked down at Dunne. "It means if we're allowed to . . . arrest . . . this man, we believe we can trade him for the location of the missing missiles."

A loud, sarcastic laugh came from Eliot West. "What he's proposing, Jim, is to kidnap a foreign national." He gave Curran a smug look. "Dirty business, Lieutenant!"

"Wouldn't that be like taking a gun and putting it to the heads of our hostages?" Elmore asked, laying the picture back on the table.

The pacing behind the desk had stopped. Stinson stared thoughtfully at Curran. "Everyone hold on for a minute. Please continue, Lieutenant Curran."

"This action will be completely nonattributable

to the United States. We'll make it look like the work of another local radical group."

The room was silent. Curran knew this was a bold plan. He looked over to Dunne for reassurance. Dunne was watching Stinson as the man resumed his pacing. A clock on Stinson's desk ticked loudly in the quiet room.

Elmore took a breath and exhaled loudly. "This may be the wrong question for this distinguished group, but do we have a moral justification for this illegal act?"

Curran was growing more frustrated with each minute that passed. Elmore's question provided him with a vent. He leaned over and placed both hands on the table. His eyes locked with Elmore's. "How's this? Fahladi's brother has been directly linked to the 1985 Vienna airport murders and the 1984 bombing of the Marine barracks. Does that give you enough moral justification?"

The loud clock continued to tick on the desk as Curran straightened back up and looked over at Warren Stinson, who had stopped pacing again. The NSC chief walked around his desk and sat down at the table next to Dunne. The pictures were scattered in front of him. Stinson gathered them up and flipped through them, then concentrated on the aerial photo. He glanced over at Dunne. "My only question is this: . . . What's the probability of success?"

With his brows knitted together and deeply furrowed, Dunne's face showed concern, but he answered confidently. "Our estimates are in the solid ninety-percent range. Lieutenant Curran, who will be the commander on the operation, figures higher."

Stinson nodded, still looking at the photographs of the two Fahladi brothers. He chewed on the inside of his cheek, deep in thought, then handed the pictures to Curran. "Gentlemen, it's in your hands. Four Stinger missiles are still unaccounted for. Be smart, but more than that, be good."

Trying to hide his satisfaction, Curran looked over at Dunne. The meeting was over for them. They excused themselves and left the conference, leaving the three civilians still seated at the table. The outside door to the White House wing had barely closed behind them when Curran startled Dunne with an uncharacteristic victory whoop. Dunne knew how much it meant to Curran to be able to vindicate his team, but he continued to walk on, frowning.

Recovering his composure, Curran noticed Dunne's face. "Hey, we have another chance at it! I would have thought you'd be as pleased as I am."

"Don't misunderstand, Curran. I'm pleased, but I'm also aware that there are only a fixed number of times we can go after those missiles. This is a big gamble, and it had better pay off."

"We'll get those missiles, sir. My team wants them more than anyone else. We can do it," Curran said, realizing, as Dunne did, that there was no room left for mistakes.

They walked on together in silence, each with his own thoughts, down Pennsylvania Avenue to the waiting sedan. When they were in the car and headed toward SEAL headquarters, Dunne picked up the mobile phone and called in a code, placing Curran's team on alert. This alert would reach all the team members, telling them to report to the SEAL briefing room as quickly as they could. He hung up the phone and turned to Curran. "Well, the ball is in your court."

Curran quickly went through his plan with Dunne in the car. As they walked into the headquarters, Captain Dunne extended his hand to Curran. "I'll get your support lined up while you brief your men. Good luck!" He shook Curran's hand, then disappeared into his office.

Curran hurried down the corridor to the briefing room. He opened the door and saw that all the members of his team were already there, impatiently waiting for him. They knew from the warning order they'd received that they were about to go.

After telling them what the mission involved, Curran went into the actual planning of the operation. Stepping over to the side of the room, he pulled down a large wall map.

"We'll stay in the commercial air lanes, drop at thirty thousand feet over international waters, open at two thousand feet, and swim to shore. Any questions so far?"

No one said anything as they watched Curran. Dane shifted in his chair, causing everyone to glance over at him, but he remained silent.

"Okay then, this is it." Curran pulled the cord on the wall map, returning it to its place, then stepped over in front of the model he'd had made of Assad Fahladi's villa. "Leary and I will go up the back wall and in through the porch on the third story. Dane and Rexer will go in through the window here." He indicated a side window on the second floor. "Graham, Ramos, and Hawkins, take the three guards out at the front entrance and secure the first floor.

Once the opposition is neutralized and the target's been taken down, we'll be exiting out that door. Hawkins, make sure the first floor is secure and clear." He glanced up from the model at the man standing next to him. "Understood?"

Hawkins nodded and looked back at the model, studying the layout of the rooms. "This is a big son of a bitch," he said, looking at the villa. "Just one family lives there?"

Leary had been in charge of researching and building the model. "Yeah," he answered, "it's just Assad, his wife, and their two kids. The wife, her servants, and the kids live on the third floor, and Assad, his bodyguards, and servants live on the second floor."

"His wife lives on the third floor?" Graham asked.

"Yeah, it seems rich Muslims don't allow their women and children in the same quarters they live in. It goes back to their days when they had big harems," Curran explained.

"Oh, yeah." Graham shuffled around for a minute. "I . . . I need to tell you guys something."

"What?" Curran asked, as he threw a cloth over the model.

"Well, Jolena and I are getting married tomorrow in D.C. by a justice of the peace."

There was a stunned silence in the room, until Hawkins let out a dramatic groan. "Oh, Graham! Do we have to cancel it for you again?"

"Not this time, and that's what Jolena is afraid of, so we decided—"

"WE decided?" Hawkins interrupted. "It sounds more like SHE decided."

Curran stepped over and shook Graham's hand. "I don't give a damn who decided. I'm happy for you, Billy. Do you want to stand down for this mission? You've certainly got some leave time coming."

"No! I want—and intend—to be a part of this mission."

"Okay." Curran smiled broadly. "But you tell Jolena I offered." He turned back to the rest of the SEALs. "After we withdraw from the target, we're extracting fast in a patrol boat painted in Lebanese colors. That's it! H-Hour is at 2100 hours. Let's get a move on."

Within the hour, Curran, Hawkins, and the rest of the team boarded a jet at the air base and began the first leg of their trip, which would take them to a launch base in the Mediterranean. Dunne had made all the calls; the support was in place and lined up.

17

The sun was just beginning to set on the tarmac at Nicosia, Cyprus, as the team made their way over to the waiting Hercules C-130 transport. Curran watched as the equipment and men loaded the plane, its big turbo prop engines making an ear-splitting whine.

Captain Dunne had accompanied them to Cyprus and now waited with Curran on the side of the runway.

"Assuming the rest of it goes okay, the big thing to worry about is the extraction. Our fast boat will be on radar the second we start in, so we only get one pass at it. If you're not on time, to the second, you'll have to hitch a ride," he warned.

"We'll be there. It's not a good place to look for a friendly ride," Curran said. He saluted Dunne, turned, and ran to the plane. Standing in the door, Leary extended a hand to Curran, helping him up into the plane. Once inside, Curran turned and looked back at Dunne, giving him a thumbs-up signal.

With the team and their equipment loaded, the two Air Force loadmasters secured the door and continued to talk to the pilot through their headsets. The plane slowly turned and began to taxi down the runway. There was a power thrust, then the wheels of the transport lifted off the ground and retracted. They were airborne, headed toward the gulf and the port at Sidon.

In the plane, the men strapped on their parachutes, checked their bail-out bottles and equipment, then settled back in the red nylon seats, talking with each other or checking their equipment one more time.

Hawkins nudged Curran and pointed over to Graham, who, as usual, was reading a book. The title was *How to Love a Woman*. They both laughed, and Graham looked up at them, smiling sheepishly. Shrugging his shoulders, he turned back to his book.

Dane sat back, his face ashen, staring straight ahead. "Where are the barf bags?" he asked, unaware that he had one in his left hand.

"Cherry jumper!" Leary said, looking over at him. "It's in your hand. What's with you?"

Dane leaned over and pulled out Leary's earplug. Speaking directly into his ear, Dane said, in his usual monotone, "I HATE to jump."

Leary laughed, retrieved the earplug, and wadded it back into his ear. "You don't gotta love it . . . you just gotta do it!"

They had been in the air for over an hour when

Curran stood up and looked out one of the tiny side windows. He knew that the moon was full, but he wasn't prepared for the brightness outside the plane.

The night sky appeared to be a deep, rich blue-black, with silver-fringed clouds floating here and there over the velvety horizon. He sat back down and tried to clear his mind of everything but the mission. He was fighting the image of Claire's deep brown eyes, filled with tears. He felt a deep, gnawing pain every time he thought of her, and he had thought of her often since their last unsatisfactory conversation.

Shaking his head to rid himself of the image, he blocked out everything except what would take place in the next few hours. Everything else would have to wait until he could deal with it . . . if there was anything left to deal with.

The C-130 climbed steadily up into the stratosphere, far above the cloud cover, and skimmed the edge of space. Up in the cockpit, the pilot spoke into his mike: "Uh, Black Fire, this is X-Ray. Come in."

Black Fire Six, an Air Force AWAC, answered from somewhere over the Mediterranean: "Go ahead, X-Ray. We are open for business."

The C-130 pilot spoke again into the mike: "Iron Rifle, this is X-Ray. AWAC has acquired . . ." The transmissions insured that all the pieces of this game were now on the board.

Back in the cargo section of the plane, the senior loadmaster started toward the ramp area in the tail, passing Rexer and Ramos. Rexer stuck out his arm to stop the man. The Air Force sergeant leaned down to hear his question.

"What's our altitude?" Rexer yelled over the noise.

"About thirty thousand feet," the loadmaster replied. "Jumping from six miles up . . . you guys are crazy!"

"Hey man, and proud of it! You can go with us!" Ramos said, smiling up at the man in the flightsuit, who shook his head while shouting "Hell, no!" back at him.

The two loadmasters made their preparations for the jump and handed a headset to Curran, who functioned as jumpmaster. Curran nodded as he established communications with the pilot of the C-130.

In the center of the plane was a large tubular metal console with two rows of regulators, each with a hose attached. A long green oxygen cylinder ran the length of the console.

"Prepare to depressurize," the pilot announced through the mike. Curran stood up and faced the men. All eyes in the plane focused on him as he pulled up one of the black hoses on the console and attached it to his pack. He turned to the jumpers and tapped his fists together, the signal for them to hook up to the oxygen console.

When each man had hooked up, he gave a thumbs-up to Curran. When everyone was on the oxygen, Curran spoke into the intercom to tell the pilot they were ready to depressurize the plane.

The only illumination inside the cavernous body of the plane were the red lights along the side, which cast a hazy glow.

Curran looked back at his team, giving each man in turn a thumbs-up. Each man returned the gesture, signaling that they were getting oxygen and okay. The pilot's voice came over the intercom again: "Ramp down."

The tail section of the C-130 seemed to fall away as the ramp opened and locked in place. Curran signaled for Leary, the first jumper in line, to disconnect from the console and move back closer to the edge of the ramp. The other SEALs followed Leary. Curran put an arm in front of him and waited, listening to the pilot in the headset and looking back over the end of the ramp. He hit Leary on the shoulder. Leary leaped out, propelling himself into the velvet darkness.

"Go! . . . Go! . . . Go! . . ." cried Curran, as the rest of the SEALs threw themselves off the ramp. As the last one went out, Curran threw off the headset and hurled himself off the ramp into the night.

The night embraced them, hiding the jumpers in the crystal stars and the fading sun, still visible from the high altitude. The men rapidly dropped away from the C-130. Rushing air drowned out all sound, and the dark-blue night became completely silent. They continued breathing through the oxygen masks for a while, then unhooked them to better read the luminous dials on their altimeters.

From its position out over the Mediterranean, the AWAC tracked them. A voice relayed their position to call-sign Iron Rifle: "Altitude twenty-eight thousand feet, airspeed a hundred and thirty knots, approaching point of deployment."

Arms and legs extended, the SEALs fell through the dark sky, watching the altimeters on their wrists. The night sky was quiet and calm, at least for everyone but Dane. He nervously watched the needle of his altimeter as it wound down to two thousand feet, and then he quickly yanked his rip cord. As the chute opened and filled, Dane swung suspended over the earth, doing a silent victory dance in midair.

Around him, the others began pulling their rip cords, the chutes exploding from their backs into square canopies. They floated together in a wedge-shaped pattern, allowing just enough space between them to avoid entanglement with each other. Curran could see each of his men as they swung from their chutes, high in the black sky over the gulf.

As they floated along under their steerable chutes, Rexer pointed down to the port area now clearly visible beneath them. The parachute descent took little more time than the thirty-thousand-foot free-fall, and soon they could see the water coming up to meet them. Each man, knowing that he was within a few feet of touchdown, prepared for a water landing. Releases were pulled upon impact, and the chutes and harnesses quickly fell away.

Watching as the men splashed in, Curran looked for each one, making sure they all popped to the surface. When they were all collected, the team started their short swim to the shore.

The voice over the mike from the AWAC reported to Iron Rifle: "Touchdown! They're on their own."

The stillness of the night was broken only by the occasional sound of the waves as the team stealthily glided through the water toward the lights on the shore. Nearing the beach, Curran suddenly held up his hand. The signal told the others to freeze. They all focused on the shoreline, looking for the threat.

Up ahead, two people strolled leisurely along the

water's edge. Curran glanced at his watch. The schedule was tight, allowing for no delays, but neither was there any provision for early detection. They continued to tread water for what seemed to be an eternity until the couple finally turned and walked away. As soon as the pair was out of sight, Curran signaled the team up out of the water.

Assad Fahladi's villa wasn't the average hovel of a starving revolutionary; it was a mini-palace, complete with a large courtyard and fountain. The downstairs portion of the house was old, originally the home of a minor sultan, built in a lavish style, with graceful curved arches embellished with delicately carved latticework.

The courtyard was tiled, and clusters of orange and lemon trees stood in large pots, providing fragrance and shade. Thick bougainvillea vines climbed over the outside walls, spreading their deep crimson blossoms everywhere. There were benches and pillows placed randomly around the fountain in this classic Arabian garden. The fountain was the focal point of the courtyard. Its large font spewed a spray about two feet high, and the water fell onto fragile ceramic disks, making a musical sound.

Several rooms in the older structure opened directly to a covered walkway around the court. The original potentate kept his harem in these rooms by the gardens. Today, the spacious rooms were used as meeting areas for various radical groups, including the Al Shuhada. The rooms were opulently decorated with silken couches and richly woven carpets. Assad Fahladi was a man who loved luxury.

The villa had been remodeled in the late 1930s, when the second and third floors had been added and all the modern amenities, like electricity and indoor plumbing, had been installed. The add-on had not been as artfully built as the original structure, but it contained the private portion of the large mansion.

There were three entrances to the villa on the first floor. The main entry was a large double door for family members and guests. Two small service entries were on the south side of the building, near the kitchen and servants' quarters.

The upper floors had large open porches on both the front, facing the harbor, and the side, overlooking the courtyard.

The team moved silently down the narrow streets, using the shadowy doorways for cover. They came to the rear of the villa and split up. Ramos, Graham, and Hawkins went over to the smallest of the service doors, while Leary, Curran, Rexer, and Dane began to scale the rear wall up to the porches.

Ramos pulled out two slender steel tools, each about the size of a large toothpick, and pushed them into the lock. He flicked one of the slim tools twice, and the door opened. The kitchen was dark and empty. The three hooded men crept across the room and moved silently through the shadows of the covered walkway.

Curran and Leary climbed easily up onto the second-floor porch, as Dane and Rexer continued past them, up to the third floor.

Rexer helped Dane over the stone railing, and they stopped by a half-open casement window. Dane reached down and gave it a shove; the window sprang open. They leaned in and climbed quietly over the sill.

Curran waited while Leary, using his glass cutter, cut a small oval in one of the French doors, then reached inside, opening the door into a darkened room. They glided noiselessly across the room and opened the door to the hallway.

Hawkins led his group across the courtyard. Ramos and Graham fanned out behind him, approaching the large foyer. Two guards squatted near the double doors, playing a dice game on the marble floor. They never saw the hooded men as Ramos took aim and shot them both with his silenced P38 pistol.

Hawkins swung around the corner of the foyer, startling the two maids and a young boy standing there folding clothes. Behind him, Ramos whispered hoarsely in Arabic for them to be silent. They nodded mutely and huddled together near the base of the large staircase.

On the second floor, Leary and Curran edged down the hallway to the master bedroom. Light poured out underneath the door of the large living quarters. They could hear the sounds of a TV and men laughing inside. Dane stood on the staircase between the floors, with Rexer on the landing of the third floor. They watched as Curran took a last look around, checked their positions, and nodded to Leary; then he stepped forward, pulling open the door to the master suite.

Assad Fahladi was lying on the bed in a white robe and turban, placidly watching a dubbed episode of *F Troop* on a big-screen color TV. Two of his bodyguards were sitting in reclining chairs, watching the show with him.

One of the guards glanced up as the door creaked

open. Still watching the TV, he rose from his chair and walked over to close the door. Just as he approached the door, it swung open wide and Curran fired a muffled two-shot burst, dropping him on the floor, then pivoted and nailed the other guard still in his chair.

Assad jerked up in the bed and flipped his legs over the side, trying to get up. Leary jumped over the body on the floor and held his gun on Assad, shaking his head at the terrified man. The turbaned Arab slid back onto his pillows, his eyes wide with fright.

"Bag him for travel," Curran said to Leary, stepping out to motion Dane into the room. Dane entered and stood menacingly in front of Assad, as Leary pulled out some plastic ties and motioned for the Arab to roll over onto his stomach. The man was too stunned and frightened to resist. He turned over passively and let the SEAL bind his hands and gag him.

Leary looked over at the TV as he worked. "God, I hate that shit," he said, nodding at the set. "*F Troop* sucks, especially in Arabic!" He finished and turned to Curran. "We're road ready."

Dane looked out to the hall and motioned for Rexer to move into the room, while he took a position on the second-floor landing. Rexer came over to the bed and helped Leary get Assad up.

Graham stood by the front door while Hawkins leaned on the staircase, looking out into the courtyard. The boy huddled with the maids as Ramos questioned them.

Ramos held out a stick of gum, offering it to the kid. The boy shook his head and buried his face in one of the women's skirt. Ramos stared at him for a minute, then reached into his pocket and pulled out a pack of Marlboros, holding them forward. The boy looked over and quickly snatched them from Ramos, rattling something in Arabic as he pushed the cigarettes into the waistband of his trousers.

"The kid says there's two more bodyguards," Ramos called softly to Hawkins.

"Shit!" Hawkins said, looking back at Ramos. "Quick, check the back rooms, NOW!" Ramos darted down the covered walkway toward the other rooms, as Hawkins charged up the stairs, leaving Graham alone at the front door. The kid was watching, waiting for an opportunity. He shoved away from the women and made a dash for the door. Graham swung out an arm to stop him, but the kid ducked underneath and scrambled past him, out the front door. Graham twisted around and plunged out into the street after him.

The boy stumbled on the step, slowing just enough for Graham to grab him. Graham threw his hand up over the boy's mouth and tried to drag the boy back to the doorway, when one of the Al Shuhada guards stepped around the corner, his gun trained on Graham.

Curran stood in the hall, watching as Rexer lifted the bound Assad up on his shoulders. Dane and Leary stood outside the room, covering the hallway, as Hawkins came rushing up the stairs. Curran turned and saw him. "What the fuck are you doing here! You're supposed to be downstairs!" As Curran spoke, gunshots from outside boomed, shattering the silence.

"Oh, shit!" Hawkins spun around and bolted back down the stairs to the foyer.

The double front doors were standing wide open. The light from the foyer spread out onto the street, revealing the prone body of Billy Graham lying in a pool of blood. The Al Shuhada gunman approached the body cautiously. As he bent over to check the man, his head jerked back violently and he collapsed to the ground. Hawkins lowered his gun, sprang out into the street, and knelt down by Graham. He turned and frantically waved to Leary, standing in the door, to come out. Leary dashed over and dropped down by Hawkins. He grabbed Graham and started searching for a pulse. Stunned, Curran rushed out to join them.

"Shit!" Leary cried, slowly putting Graham's arm down. He looked up into Curran's wide eyes. "He's dead," he said softly.

Curran stared down at his friend. "No!" he whispered, knowing that it was true.

Hawkins stood up, his face frozen in shock. "My God!"

Curran began to recover and looked down at his watch. "We've got five minutes. Extract. NOW!"

Everyone began to move except Hawkins, who hovered over the dead man in the street. Curran grabbed the front of his shirt and whirled him around. "I said NOW! You move it, Hawkins!"

Hawkins stared blankly at him, slowly coming out of shock. "What about Graham?" he asked, looking down at the body lying at his feet.

Curran brusquely pushed Hawkins out of the way, bent down, and pulled Graham's body up onto his shoulders. He began to run down the street toward the water. The others, with Assad Fahladi in tow, dashed after him. They ran down the street to the docks and inflated the rubber boat Dane had carried in his large bundle.

The Zodiac inflated quickly and they climbed in, yanking Fahladi in with them and positioning him between Rexer and Dane. The soundless motor started, and they moved out into the harbor. Curran stood in the boat, next to Graham's body, guarding him in death as Hawkins had failed to do in life.

Hawkins stood next to Curran and continued to stare at the lifeless form as the waves buffeted the boat, causing Graham's head to bump against the deck. Hawkins knelt down and held the dead man's head to keep it still. He looked into Graham's still face and ran his hand over the frozen features. Curran glanced down, watching him. He clenched his jaw and stared back into the night. The destroyer loomed up in the darkness, ready to pull them from the dark sea.

18

As soon as the C-141 touched down at Norfolk, Curran left the group and drove down to his houseboat. He took a quick shower, dressed, then got back in his jeep and headed for the Norfolk Nursery. The jeep glided into a parking place near the door to one of the giant potting sheds.

Curran sat in the vehicle, dreading what he had to do. Finally he opened the door and stepped out onto the pavement. Squaring his shoulders, he walked into the vast greenhouse.

In the rear of the building were a series of tables all cluttered with planting soil, red clay pots in assorted sizes, and various types of bulbs. A group of women worked at each table, sorting the bulbs and stacking pots. Jolena was by herself at the far end of one of the tables, concentrating on her work, as Curran made his way over.

She was placing tiny bulbs in each of the pots, covering them with a dark mixture of peat moss and earth, when she heard footsteps behind her. Turning, she wiped her hands on the back of her jeans and smiled with surprise, as she recognized the man walking toward her. He drew nearer, and she could see the expression on his face. Her smile faded quickly. Her shoulders slumped forward and her face fell. She knew what he was going to say even before Curran could speak. Her head flew back with an agonized cry and she began to sob. Curran put his arms around her and pulled her close. He spoke in quiet, broken tones, his lips tenderly brushing her hair as he held her.

Thin, infinite lines of white tombstones spread out across the hallowed grounds of Arlington National Cemetery. The slow procession of cars came to a halt behind the dark hearse. The sky was dark and overcast with large, threatening clouds overhead.

The casket was placed over an open plot, and the small group of people took their places under the canopy set up for the graveside service. The SEAL task force, in dress blues, stood in rows next to the flag-draped coffin. Curran, Hawkins, and Dunne stood at one end of the casket, facing the family members, who were being seated. Allowing Ramos to assist her, Jolena sat in the center of the family. She looked like a crushed rag doll, with dark circles lining her swollen eyes. Her face looked as if it were made of stone, emotionless and painfully empty.

Curran involuntarily flinched as she glanced up at him, holding his eyes for a moment, then looking back down at the casket. He noticed she had Graham's gold class ring in her hand, clasping and unclasping it in her fist.

Lightning cut a ragged zigzag across the dark, heavy sky, followed by a clap of thunder. The chaplain concluded his service, his voice droning over the crowd: "And so take this noble warrior, who gave his life in defense of his country's values and beliefs, in defense of his fellow brethren's freedom, into your all-consuming spirit and everlasting light. May he rest in eternal peace. Amen."

"Amen," murmured the crowd in response, as the prayer ended.

The drill captain spoke softly, and seven riflemen raised their weapons. The shots rang out three times, and each time they fired, Jolena's shoulders jerked.

Before the last report had faded, a distant bugler began to play Taps. The sad melody drifted over the rows of white tombstones to the people standing at the fresh grave.

Taps is so final, thought Curran, as the last note hung in the air. Curran had been looking at the casket in front of him as the bugler played. He felt someone staring at him and looked up into Hawkins's eyes. They exchanged dark looks, full of anger and hurt.

Leary removed the flag from Graham's casket. He and Rexer folded it neatly into a triangle and handed it to Curran, who turned on his heel, took three steps forward, and stood before Graham's mother at attention. His lips barely moved as he said the words that traditionally accompany the presentation of the flag to a loved one. The words were at once both deeply moving and strangely impersonal. ". . . Accept this flag as a token from a grateful nation." As he placed the flag in her hands, their eyes locked, and he felt his own pain mix with hers.

The service concluded. Several people stopped to speak to Jolena as they walked out to their cars. The crowd moved away, leaving Curran standing by Jolena. She reached out and caressed the corner of the gray metal casket, then turned to walk away. Curran took her arm, and they walked down the grassy slope together. A light mist began to fall.

"The truth"—Jolena's voice was husky and tired—"I have a right to know. How did he die?"

He knew the question was coming but was still unprepared. "I told you. It was a training accident."

"Bullshit!" Jolena sighed, continuing to walk along. "You're lying, Curran."

The pain in her voice was almost unbearable. "I'm sorry, Jolena," he said, wishing desperately that this had not happened, that he wasn't standing there lying to her.

She stopped and stared stonily up at him. "You can take all that classified, unsung-hero CRAP and shove it!" Tears sprang from her eyes, and she began to sob. Curran put his arm around her.

"Oh, God, Curran. He's gone!" she sobbed. "He really thought . . . he thought I was beautiful!"

Curran held her closer, feeling the racking shudders of Jolena's body as she broke down, her world shattered.

As soon as she had regained some control, he walked her down to the waiting limousine and helped her inside. The dark car pulled away from the curb and headed back to Norfolk.

Curran waited until the car was out of sight, then walked back up to Graham's grave. He stood there as the rain began to come down, softly at first, then in torrents. Curran continued his silent vigil until two men appeared to finish covering the grave. They watched as he snapped a salute over the grave and turned quickly, walking down the road to his waiting jeep.

19

The drive from Arlington to Norfolk was automatic; Curran was completely involved in his own thoughts as the jeep cruised through the traffic. He took a mental inventory of everything he had in his life and came to the sharp realization that he didn't have much. He was angry—with himself, with the system, with everything in general—and depressed by the empty, hollow existence he was living.

Graham had been his best friend. He had always been so quick to tell Graham what to do, what he needed. Funny how he had been able to guide Graham so easily, when he himself moved so restlessly from one thing to another, never realizing his own needs, never making a commitment, never making a compromise, never letting anyone get to him. Except Graham.

Now he was gone, irretrievably gone, but Curran still remembered his wide smile and his unquestioning friendship and loyalty. They had been together from the first, through it all, from training to Beirut to Nicaragua. Everything.

The empty space inside would never be filled. Graham had left this space in him and in Jolena, and Curran wondered, as he drove down the beach to Ramos's house, who would feel an empty space if he left. The answer almost crushed him as he pulled up and stopped in front of the ramshackle beach house. Unbidden, the anger began to return as he stepped out of the jeep and wandered up to the door.

He smiled as he recognized the music booming out over the speakers, onto the beach. It was "Too Young," and incredible oldie by Nat King Cole. He walked up the sandy walkway onto a wooden porch that badly needed repairs. The music was so loud it formed a physical barrier as Curran approached the door.

Dane sat on the floor, nursing a bottle of tequila and looking through one of the old issues of *Playboy* magazine that littered the room. He glanced up as Curran walked in and raised the bottle in greeting. "Hi, boss. Have a swallow," he said, extending the José Cuervo to him.

Accepting the bottle, Curran took a swallow of the golden liquid, enjoying the rippling warmth and bite of the tequila. "Thanks," he said, handing the bottle back to Dane. "Where's Ramos?"

Dane waved the bottle back toward the rear of the house and continued to leaf through the magazines. Curran stepped over him and headed toward the kitchen. He moved through a crowd of people, many of whom he'd never seen before, on his way through the room. The loud music fought with the alcohol-fueled voices and nervous laughter around him.

He made his way into a cluttered living area, where he found Rexer plopped on a rickety couch next to a beerkeg. The hose from the keg was in his mouth, a makeshift demand regulator rigged to the nozzle. He held a plastic laser gun and fired at the running dots of a video game that flashed on the television screen.

"Too Young" had finished, and Nat King Cole's voice began to warble "Secret Love" from the big stereo system in the corner.

"Jeezus, Ramos!" Leary drunkenly shouted, swinging a half-full bottle of champagne. "Graham would puke in his shoes if he knew we were playing this shit at his wake! He liked to rock!" Leary gyrated his hips around, almost falling over. A thin redhead sitting in the rattan princess chair near him stood up, and the two of them began to sway around the room.

Ramos leaned against the wall, his eyes at half-mast, as he watched Leary and the girl dance. He lifted his own bottle to his lips and took a deep gulp. "Hey man!" he yelled across the room to Leary. "You don't know DICK about Graham. Nat King Cole was his favorite singer!"

Leary stopped dancing and grabbed the girl, leading her over to the cassette player. "Let's see if we can find some real music, baby!" he said, knocking over a box of tapes that clattered noisily on the floor.

"You touch that fucking stereo, Leary, and I'll rip off your balls!" Ramos yelled, starting toward him.

"Oh yeah!" Leary tossed the girl over to the side.

"Well, let's see if you can." He prepared to meet Ramos, when Curran jumped between them.

"Why don't you both just shut the fuck up!" Curran said, pushing them apart.

Leary teetered back and forth on his heels as he stared at the man standing between him and Ramos. "Why don't you sit on this?" Leary said, holding out the bottle to Curran. Then with a sudden fury, he heaved it at the picture window.

The bottle hit the window with a loud bang and the glass exploded, sending slivers flying around the room. One of the women screamed, then began to laugh nervously. The only sounds in the room were Nat King Cole's singing and her fading, hysterical laugh.

Ramos stood still for a moment. "This is my home, man!" he yelled at Leary. "Don't you have respect for private property?" He staggered over, swinging his bottle back and forth in the air. "I'm the only one's got a right to trash this place." With that, he threw his bottle through another of the windows.

No one moved. Then, suddenly, both men looked at each other, slapped palms, and started to laugh. The others joined in the mad laughter, all except Curran. A loud pounding on the door interrupted the laughter.

Ramos weaved his way over to see who it was. Standing in the open doorway was a short, heavy man in his midforties. The blue polo shirt he was wearing barely covered his bulging beer gut. He impatiently tapped one of his Gucci-clad feet on the porch and adjusted his horn-rimmed glasses as he looked disgustedly into the house.

Ramos recognized him. "Hey, you live next door, right! Come on in, man, and have a drink." He slurred as he reached out to the agitated man in the doorway.

The man slammed both hands on his hips indignantly as he spoke through tightly pursed lips. "Hardly! There are some responsible people around here who have to get up in the morning and go to work!"

Staggering over to join Ramos, Leary swung his arm toward the room. "Oh, come on in and hoist one up." He reached down and picked up the bottle next to Dane and took a swallow.

"I don't drink on weekdays!" the man said, pushing the bottle away when Leary extended it to him. "Not all of us have the luxury to drink and carouse whenever we feel like it!" His high-pitched voice took on a sneering, self-righteous tone.

This statement provoked laughter and hoots from the crowd. Dane, still sitting on the floor, drunkenly tried to focus his eyes on the man in the door. Suddenly he stood up, wobbling back and forth, and pointed to the disgusted little man. "He looks like a yuppie! I hate yuppies!" he said loudly, in his deep monotone.

Having abandoned his beerkeg and video game to see what was happening, Rexer stepped over to Dane and lowered his arm. "Cool it!" he said to Dane.

Ramos was shaking his head. "Look, man, I'm sorry," he said to the irate neighbor. "This is a wake. We lost a good buddy and—"

The man was not interested in what Ramos was saying. He raised his arm and shook his fist. "Well, your wake is keeping me from my sleep. If this

179

racket doesn't stop by the time I get back to my place, I'm calling the police."

As he lowered his arm and turned to go, Hawkins, who had been sitting quietly in a chair the whole time, suddenly sprang to his feet. "Hey!" he yelled to the departing man. The man turned back around as Hawkins stomped toward him.

"Yeah, buttface, I'm talking to you!" said Hawkins, stepping up and jabbing a finger into the startled man's face. "While you were spit-polishing your BMW, our comrade-in-arms was laying down his life to defend you, so you could have a house to sleep in. . . . So, shithead, if we happen to keep you up a few extra hours, that's just too goddamned bad!"

Hawkins gave him a shove, which sent the man spinning off the porch, then turned around and slammed the door.

Everyone in the room screamed with approval, giving Hawkins a high-five as he stepped away from the door. Ramos grabbed a can of beer from a blonde standing nearby, shook it up, and sprayed Hawkins with it.

Wiping the beer away and laughing, Hawkins stepped over to the table, popped a bottle of champagne, and held it up. "To Graham!" he said solemnly. "The best friend a man could have." Everyone but Curran joined in. Curran stared at Hawkins with revulsion, then turned and walked out the door.

A strong wind whipped up off the water, scattering the light sprinkle of rain. Curran stood on the end of the porch, letting the rain blow in his face and watching the lights blinking across the harbor. Hawkins walked out the door and looked around.

He stood still for a minute as he peered through the mist at Curran.

"Hey, James, it's raining, or hadn't you noticed?" he said playfully.

Ignoring him, Curran continued to stare out at the harbor as the rain came down harder and harder. Hawkins walked down to him and looked out over the water, leaning against the porch railing. There was a long silence; then Hawkins said, "What's wrong, Curran? My toast not good enough for you?"

Curran spun around and hit Hawkins in the face with a straight right hand. It caught him off guard, and Hawkins dropped to the porch floor like a rock. Curran stood over him, trembling with rage. "There, you have it!" he growled down at Hawkins.

Hawkins rubbed his jaw, shook his head, and smiled. "All right, boss," he said, bounding to his feet. "Let's get it on." His feet shot out as he threw a vicious combination of kicks and punches that sent Curran crashing through the porch railing.

Curran tumbled out onto the rain-soaked sand. He staggered up onto his feet, surprised. The torrential downpour streaked blood from the cut on his mouth. Hawkins jumped over the splintered porch rail, stepping out in front of him. He swung his arm menacingly toward Curran.

"You're not up to it, old man!" Hawkins said, planting his feet in the sand.

Curran lunged foward, hammering Hawkins with a trained boxer's left hook-right hook-left hook combination and driving him over a picnic table. Curran dove over on the top of the table as Hawkins threw up a leg and kicked him off. Hawkins leaped up on his feet and watched as Curran lay there, getting his breath back.

Pulling himself up, Curran turned on him again, but this time Hawkins was ready. He unloaded a flurry of kicks and chops that sent Curran reeling.

Curran shook his head and stood, steadying himself. He held his fist up, blazing his rage at Hawkins. "You fuckin' hot dog! You sorry piece of shit! Why'd you go and leave that front door uncovered? Lookin' for a fight? Lookin' for a rush?" He lashed out with a right hook.

Hawkins dodged the swing but landed one of his own on the side of Curran's eye, opening up a new cut. "Come on, boss. Get it out of your system. The kid said there were two more guards. I thought you guys were in trouble!" He spun around, a hard kick missing Curran by inches.

They hurled themselves at each other, falling to the ground in a tight clench, rolling back and forth in the wet sand and mud, each trying to get enough leverage to land a punch on the other.

A bright beam of light spilled out onto the yard as the door opened. Most of the people who had been in the house came out onto the porch and stared out into the rain.

Curran dragged himself to his feet and stared down at Hawkins. He was breathing heavily, his chest heaving in and out. It was hard to tell who was hurt worse; both men had blood and sand smeared all over them. "Think about it, Hawk. You weren't where you were supposed to be. Graham didn't give a fuck about your rush! He just wanted to come back, that's all."

Hawkins continued to lie there, rain pelting his face, as he stared up at Curran.

"What's going on out there?" yelled Leary through the downpour.

Turning away, Curran stumbled to his jeep. He flipped on the lights and gunned the accelerator, sending the vehicle spinning erratically down the beach road. The disappearing taillights straightened out, and the people on the porch watched as the jeep disappeared into the night.

Hawkins wearily pushed himself up from the ground and wiped his face with a dirty sleeve. "Nothing!" he yelled over his shoulder. "Curran and I slipped and fell. Guess it's time we both went home." He walked out to his car. About to jump over the side of the GTO, he paused for a moment, then opened the door. He turned back to the crowd on the porch. "I suggest you all close it down and get some sleep," he said solemnly. With that, he started the car and pulled slowly out onto the drive, heading for home.

"Is that Hawk talking?" Ramos turned to Leary. "Close it down? . . . Man, he's beginning to sound just like Curran."

Rexer watched as Hawkins and his GTO disappeared down the shoreline. "He's right. The wake is over. Let's get out of here."

The crowd began to disperse. Thirty minutes later, the house was quiet and the lights were out.

20

Curran pulled into his parking place at the marina. Turning the side-view mirror around, he surveyed the damage. His left eye was swelling rapidly. By morning, it would be swollen shut. The cut on his lip didn't look serious, but his nose was still bleeding. He pulled some tissues from the glove box, threw his head back, and held them over his nose. He slowly climbed out of the jeep, one hand on his nose and the other holding his side, and began to walk down the dock past the other houseboats. He tossed the bloody tissue into the water and walked up the ramp to his door.

A figure moved in the shadows, catching his eye as he swung over onto the deck of his boat. He turned and looked. Surprise flickered across his swollen face. Claire Verens stood there in a yellow raincoat, a floppy hat pulled tightly over her head. She had obviously been standing there for some time. The wide-brimmed hat was soaked, and rivulets of rain water were pouring from the folds. Shadows fell across their faces, hiding their expressions from each other.

Curran slumped over the rail of the boat, looking down into the water. "Okay, what do you want?" he asked brusquely.

Her voice was low and restrained. "I want to talk."

Curran turned and pushed past her. "I'm not in the mood."

She continued to stand there in the rain, looking at him, as he pulled out a key and jammed it into the lock on his front door.

"You did it, didn't you?" she said softly, her voice trembling with emotion. "You kidnaped Fahladi."

He pushed the door open and stood with both hands braced against the frame. "Leave me alone." He took a deep breath and stepped inside, kicking the door shut as he walked in. Claire pushed the door open and walked in behind him.

Not bothering to turn on the lights, Curran dropped onto his couch. Claire peered though the darkness, trying to locate him. Her voice echoed the hurt and anger she was feeling inside. "I feel compromised and used. And I don't like that feeling."

There was a slight rustle on the couch. "There's nothing I could say that would make you feel better." Curran's voice was quiet and hollow.

Claire reached over on the wall and found a switch. A floorlamp came to life, spreading light on the couch and the figure seated on it. She gasped when she saw him. "My God, what happened to you?"

Curran reached over and flipped the light back off. He pulled himself up into a sitting position on the couch. "Please, Claire, this is not the time. Just leave."

She pulled her soggy hat off and laid it down on the table in the darkness. There was just enough light for her to see the profile of the man on the couch. He began to shiver. Claire watched as he reached up and pulled a blanket from the back of the couch, lay back, and curled himself tightly into it.

Claire slid the wet coat off her shoulders and laid it outside the door, then walked over to the couch. She hesitated a moment, as if trying to make up her mind. Then she sat down beside him.

"Who was it?" she asked, her voice reaching out to him across their void of silence. "Who did you lose out there?"

He lay very still on the couch, fighting for control. "I'd really appreciate it if you'd leave. I NEED to be alone. Please, just go away."

"I'm not leaving." She reached down and stroked his shoulder. "Who was it?"

He kicked his feet over the side of the couch and sat up. Turning to speak to her, his voice caught in his throat. "It was Graham. . . . I lost Graham," he choked out.

"Oh, no . . ."

The day Curran had shown her the training area, he had spoken frequently of Graham. She knew that Graham had been as close to Curran as anyone was allowed to get. She could feel the loneliness in him and understood it. It was a feeling she'd had for over five years now, since she'd heard that the last person she knew in Beirut was dead.

Reaching over, she gently put her hand on Curran's face. "You're hurt. We need to clean you up."

He nodded absently as she got up and went over to the wall panels. She felt around until she found the switch. An overhead lamp flashed on, bathing the starkly furnished room in light.

She looked around, astonished at how little was in the room. There were no paintings hanging from the walls, no souvenirs on shelves, no reflection of the man who sat huddled on the couch, clutching a Navy blanket around himself. Maybe it tells me everything, she thought. Maybe this is a perfect picture of emptiness.

She walked toward what appeared to be the bedroom of the houseboat. It was neat and clean; everything in its place and put away. The furnishings looked as though they'd been acquired from a Navy surplus store. The bed was a narrow bunk built into the wall. Training manuals were neatly stacked at the foot of the bed.

She opened a small door into the bathroom. Again, the Spartan cleanliness struck her. Nothing was out of place. Everything seemed to be kept in a tidy, military manner. All of his shaving gear was lying on a shelf as if it had been arranged for display.

Claire turned on the hot-water tap and reached up into the medicine cabinet, looking for hydrogen peroxide and a tube of antibiotic salve. She took a washcloth from the stack near the sink and soaked it in the hot water. Turning off the tap, she gathered the first-aid things and returned to the living room. Curran sat on the couch, bent forward, holding his head between his hands.

When he heard her approaching, he straightened

up and tried to smile. "Look, this really isn't necessary. I can take care of myself," he said, watching her as she sat down beside him.

"Uh-huh, I see." She dabbed at the cut below his eye. "You've done a hellova job so far."

Curran stared blankly into the room as she wiped his face, not wincing as she treated the cuts. His voice had a faraway sound to it as he spoke. "In Beirut, the SEALs only had MREs, so we'd usually try to eat breakfast over at the Marine barracks. Graham and I were passing the gatehouse when we first heard this rumbling, screeching sound. We turned around and saw a truck charging toward us. We had nowhere to go, so we jumped back against the fence, and then"—he pulled the blanket closer—"the world shook."

Claire laid the cloth on the floor and took one of his hands into hers. "It must have been horrible."

He continued on, as if he hadn't heard her. "I can't get it out of my mind. The driver's face . . . he was smiling. He's about to blow himself up with two hundred and fifty Marines, and he's smiling." He paused, and his body began to tremble. "I've just seen too much . . . too many dead bodies. . . ."

Claire put her arm around him and pulled him closer. He held onto her as he continued to shake spasmodically. The rain had stopped; outside, the night was still, as they sat on the couch, locked in a tight embrace.

Finally, she pushed away and stood up. "Look, Curran, you're filthy. It's senseless to clean your cuts when the rest of you is covered in sand and dirt. Get out of your clothes. I think you need to get in the shower first." She reached down to help him up.

"Why are you here? I mean, you already said what you came to say. . . . Why did you stay?" He grabbed her hand and held it, looking deeply into her dark eyes.

"I don't know." She lowered her eyes and looked at the things she had gathered to work on his face.

He released her hand and stood up. "If I go take a shower, will you still be here when I get out?"

She nodded, avoiding his eyes. "Yes, but will it make a difference?"

"I think it will," he said, his hand reaching out to her face and stroking her cheek.

Curran turned and walked toward the bathroom, pulling off his soiled shirt. He closed the door behind him and sat down on the toilet seat to remove his shoes. What in the hell are you doing, Curran? he asked himself. She sees things differently than you do. There's no chance here. She's just waiting till you get your shit together. Then you're going to get one hell of a lecture about what you've done.

He pulled his shoes off and placed them by the door, then yanked off his socks and trousers and laid them by the sink. Reaching over, he hit the shower tap and watched the steaming water as it shot out across the stall. He slipped off his shorts, stepped inside, and pulled the curtain.

Lifting the soap bar from the dish, he worked a lather into his hands. His bruised and battered body slowly relaxed under the warm jets of water as he scrubbed away the sand and caked blood.

A gust of cool air swept across his back as the shower curtain opened. He turned around, his back against the shower head. Claire stood naked before him, her skin glowing as she looked up at him. "I thought maybe I'd scrub your back, if you'd scrub mine."

His arms quickly closed around her as he pulled her closer and kissed her. Curran held her away from him and looked at her. She had small, firm breasts, with dark, upturned nipples. Claire's waist was small, rolling gently into the slope of her hips. Her body was truly beautiful, dark, exotic, and flawless. Smiling, she pulled him close and kissed him again, but this time the kiss was more than tender; there was an intensity to the embrace, a passion. She pressed her body next to his, their mutual need pulling them together. The water splashed hard against his back as he slid his hands over her breasts and held them briefly, then began to stroke the firmness of her waist and hips.

As he pulled her nearer, she teased him with small kisses on his shoulders and arms. Taking one of his hands up to her mouth, Claire pressed each fingertip to her lips. He reached around behind him and turned off the shower. With one quick movement, he picked her up and held her in his arms. She slipped her arms around his neck and laid her head on his shoulder as he carried her into the bedroom.

Curran gently laid Claire on the bed, then bent over her and kissed her stomach, moving his lips over her skin up to the nipple of her left breast. She kept her hands on his shoulders and pulled him over onto the bed with her. He rolled over on his side and held her close. "Do you know what you're doing?" he said, nuzzling her breast. "Is this what you want?"

She groaned as he continued to kiss and nibble her breasts. "Shut up, Curran!" she said, as she kicked the books off the foot of the bed and rolled over on top of him, slipping his rigid hardness up between her warm, wet thighs. Straddling him, Claire sat up slowly, enjoying the feel of his shaft as it moved deeper into her. With a sigh, she leaned forward, straightening her legs next to his, and pulled him over on top of her. He looked down into her wide eyes and rocked gently over her. She moaned softly and tossed her head from side to side. He buried his face in her hair, deeply inhaling the scent of roses and cinnamon that was so much a part of her. Curran felt the sudden urgency and thrust deeply into her, feeling her move beneath him. He stiffened and cried out, "Oh, God, Claire!" As he climaxed, she arched her back and moaned, her face glowing with the ecstasy of her own orgasm. He pulled her shoulders up, almost lifting her into a sitting position, as he crushed her to him.

Lowering her back down onto the soggy sheets, he reached over and pulled a pillow under her head. She looked up at him, a smile spreading across her face.

"Hey," she said, breathlessly, "that's not bad for two people in a hurry. Can we have a rematch and take our time?"

He laughed softly and pulled a strand of her hair from her face. "Any time, lady, any time." He rolled over and started to get up.

"Whoa, sailor! Where are you going?" she asked, raising up on one elbow.

"I just happen to have a bottle of St. Emilion in my wine rack. You do like Bordeaux, don't you?"

"I love Bordeaux, especially St. Emilion. How did you know?" she asked, surprised.

"When I didn't think I'd be able to meet you any other way, I called your editor. She's a pretty talky lady. She told me a lot about you, including the fact that you liked the red wines from Bordeaux." He stopped and turned around, facing her. "I bought the bottle to give you as a bribe." He smiled and continued toward the kitchen.

"I already accepted the pencils. So why bring it out now? You know I can't tell you any more," she said, sitting up in the bed.

"It's not information I want from you now. . . . Stay where you are, I'm coming back."

Curran pulled out the bottle of wine and removed the cork. He realized, with some embarrassment, that he didn't have any wine glasses. Picking up two coffee cups, he wiped them with a washcloth, wrapped the cloth around the bottle, and returned to the bedroom. He placed the cups on his dresser, poured the wine into them, and handed one to Claire.

She smiled up at him as she accepted it. She moved over as he sat down on the bed next to her. She took a sip, then looked over at him. "Ummm, not only St. Emilion, but an excellent one, thank you." She lowered the cup and kissed him. "Now that we're lovers," she said, looking into Curran's eyes, "can we become friends?"

"I hope so." Curran took a sip of his wine, stretched, and then leaned back against the wall, an arm wrapped around her shoulders. "Where do we start?"

"Tell me about you." She curled closer to him, holding the cup in both hands.

"There's not much to tell. I was born here, in Norfolk. My dad's a career man. Mom died when I was in junior high. Dad put me in a boarding school while he did his thing around the world. I got accepted to San Diego State, finished there, got married, finished that, and here I am. . . . No big deal." He took a big swallow of the tangy red wine and held it in his mouth for a minute, savoring it.

"Where's your dad now?" Claire asked, as she slowly ran her hand over his stomach and legs.

"He's in Hawaii. Retired and remarried. He and his new wife have a girl . . . maybe two by now."

"You have two sisters! . . . What are they like?"

"I don't know. I've never seen them. . . . Well, never in person. Dad sent pictures."

"Do you see him much?" she asked, sipping the wine.

"I haven't seen him in six years. He and I don't seem to have much to say to each other . . . and we're both pretty busy." Curran was becoming uncomfortable with the conversation. "How about you."

"You already know about me. After I left Beirut, I went to live with some family friends in Paris. My folks said they were going to join me." She paused and held the cup with both hands, looking into the deep red liquid. "I think they really intended to, but it didn't work out that way. We had money in Switzerland and France. I used it to go to school, first at Harvard, then a couple of years in France. I did some time as a foreign correspondent with Associated

Press, then Reuters. Quit after a while so I could do some writing on my own."

"No husband?" Curran asked, rubbing her shoulders.

"Didn't have time." She sat up in the bed. "There were a few hurried affairs thrown in here and there but nothing I couldn't walk away from." Claire, too, was uncomfortable with the conversation. "How can you live like this, Curran? I mean, everything in here looks like it was issued to you."

He was silent for a minute, and he reached over for the wine bottle and refilled their cups. "I don't know. How can you live in a house filled with pictures of dead people?"

"Ouch!" she said. "That hurt!"

He sat up and pulled her to him. "I didn't mean for it to. We're a perfect pair, aren't we? We both have our careers, our professions. We're busy people, but neither one of us has a life." They sat there in the darkness, sipping their wine in silence.

Claire handed him her cup and stood up, stretching, her arms reaching up for the ceiling. Then she turned and started to walk away.

"Where are you going?" Curran asked, still sitting there holding the coffee cups in his hands.

"I'm going to complete that shower we started. You promised to scrub my back."

He watched her walk into the bathroom and turn on the light, moving smoothly and sensuously across his room. Soon the sound of the shower came on, and he heard her as she pulled the curtain back. Rolling off the bed, he walked in to join her.

"Room service!" he called out, as he yanked on the curtain.

Claire poked her head out of the shower. "I didn't order room service, but . . ."

He raised a cup to her lips. Claire took a sip and looked at him. "Ummm, that's good. So are you. Get in here."

He put the cups down on the sink and stepped into the shower. She leaned up and kissed him. "Now, my back, please, and I'll return the favor."

She turned her back to him as he took the soap from her. With both hands on her back, he ran the bar over her shoulders. He reached around, nudging her breasts, as he returned the soap.

Massaging the soap over her shoulders blades, he could feel the light muscles of her back. "I'm not sure I can be completely technical," he said, as his hand slid around her waist and he pressed her close to him.

She gave a low moan and stepped back, pushing herself even closer to him. He had recovered from their earlier lovemaking and felt the blood coursing through him, causing him to harden against her.

She felt him, too, and turned to face him. Her hair was plastered against her face as warm water cascaded over them.

"Your turn," she said, smiling up at him as she put her hands on his waist and turned him around. He swung around in the shower and felt her hands as they began to gently work on his back, making the soreness disappear. She continued to knead his muscles, and Curran felt himself becoming more aroused. Her hands caressed and moved over his hips, and she tugged at him, making him turn around and face her. "You're right! It is hard to remain technical," she said, as she began to lather his stomach.

"This is good. I think I could let you do this forever," he said, trying to ignore her hands. "Want another swallow of wine?"

"I think we're going to have to get out of here now," she said, putting the soap down. "I think we're out of hot water."

"This will never do," Curran said, beginning to feel the water cooling. He held the curtain for her as she stepped out. "We'll have to get a place with a monster hot-water tank." He reached around to turn off the tap. She took the towel and slowly blotted the water from his body, then she leaned up and began to kiss his shoulders, running her lips and tongue over his chest. She stopped and looked up at him. "Now I want to make slow, deliberate love with you . . . my friend."

Later, they slept peacefully in the bunk bed, curled together comfortably in each other's arms. The wine bottle lay empty beside the bed, next to two empty cups. Towels were scattered from the bed to the bathroom.

Curran woke first, lying still for several minutes, as he enjoyed the warmth of Claire's body next to his. He tried to open his eyes and discovered that his left eye was indeed swollen shut. He turned his head so he could see her face. She was waking, too, her dark eyelashes beginning to flutter softly against her cheek. He leaned over and kissed her forehead.

Her eyes opened slowly. She smiled up into his face. "God, Curran, you're a mess. I hope I didn't do that."

"No, you didn't mess up my face, just my priorities." He ran a finger over her lips, tracing their shape deep into his memory.

"Hey, we just made love! . . . It doesn't change anything." She looked at him, waiting for him to speak.

"You know damned well that things have changed. We will both go back and do our jobs. We have to, but whether we like it or not, things have changed." He continued to stroke her face.

She smiled and reached up, pulling his face down to meet hers in a deep, passionate kiss. "I hoped you'd say that."

Curran pulled her hand up from the sheets and began to move his lips over her palm, down her wrists, and to the curve of her elbow. She groaned and shuddered as she ran her hands over his body. They moved closer, easing their bodies together.

21

Several thousand miles from Norfolk, the scene was quite different. There were no sparkling lights swinging over the harbor, only the jagged, jarring skyline of Beirut. The city that had once been the proud example for all Middle East cities, a harmonious blend of Muslims, Christians, and Jews, was now a bombed-out ruin. It held no beauty, no sparkle of enlightenment, no sign of the great culture that had once flourished there.

There were isolated explosions in the distance and the sounds of sporadic artilleryfire. Children and women huddled together in the streets, hungry and terrified. A siren wailed as an ambulance bounced down a narrow street, threading its way through the rubble.

Ben Shaheed watched from the window of a half-ruined building as the ambulance passed by. He turned around and faced the four Arabs sitting around the table. His voice was hard like steel and just as cold. "We must speed up the training. The missiles must be dispersed."

A thin, bearded man in a ragged turban leaned forward. "We have enthusiasm," he said to Shaheed, "but few qualified trainers."

Shaheed listened to the man while he calmly studied his hands. "Then," he answered quietly, "you must double your efforts. Even Western intelligence sometimes gets lucky."

Shaheed shifted his gaze to Amal Fahladi, a porcine man with angry eyes, who stared at him across the table. With a wave of his hand, he ended the discussion and dismissed the others. "That will be all."

As the men rose and walked to the door, Shaheed approached Fahladi. He reached over and put his hand on his shoulder. "I'm sorry about your brother."

Fahladi turned and looked at him, his eyes bright with anger. "Who did it?" he asked.

"We suspect the Phalange," Shaheed answered, his face darkening, "but perhaps not."

Fahladi nodded and started down the stairs. Shaheed stared after the man as he stepped past the guards at the door out into the street.

Fahladi climbed into the back seat of his Mercedes Benz 350SE and motioned to the driver. A bodyguard carrying an AK47 sat in the passenger seat. The sleek black car slowly made its way down the street.

The car bumped over the rubble-strewn streets. As it turned the corner, a Chevrolet Impala pulled up alongside. Gunmen fired their Uzis into the Mercedes, instantly killing the driver and the bodyguard in the front seat. The Mercedes rolled forward over a mound of dirt, almost overturning.

Three gunmen jumped out of the Chevrolet and ran over to the Mercedes, yanking the door open. Inside, Amal Fahladi cowered on the floor. The gunmen pulled him out and threw him into the Chevy. The driver of the Impala hit the gas, and the car squealed away.

They sped rapidly down the streets, careening around corners, then screeching to a stop in front of the ruins of an old church. The gunmen jumped out and pulled a sobbing, blubbering Amal Fahladi with them, snatching him into the church as the car roared away.

Fahladi was tied up and gagged. Several hours later, a man in a burnoose entered the baptistery in which Fahladi was being held. He spoke quickly to the guards in Hebrew, then stepped over to where Fahladi was propped against the wall. He smiled and removed the gag from Fahladi's mouth. The prisoner's eyes bulged with fear.

"Hello, Banker Fahladi," the man said, switching to Arabic. "If you ever wish to see your brother again, you will give us the information we need." Before the man in the burnoose could finish speaking, there was an Uzi muzzle pressed to Fahladi's sweating groin.

Curran and Claire stood over a chopping block in the tiny kitchen. He wore a pair of gray sweatpants. Claire's bare legs extended from his sweatshirt with the "NAVY" logo printed across the chest.

"You're sure you know how to make Western

omelets?" Claire asked, as she cut julienne strips from a green pepper.

"Who do you think does the cooking around here?" He peeled the skin off a large purple onion and waited for Claire to hand him the knife.

"Humm," she said, handing over the paring knife. "I hope the omelet is better than your coffee." She picked up a piece of pepper and took a bite.

"What's wrong with the coffee?"

"It tastes like bilgewater." She held the slice of pepper up for him to taste.

"Well, if you don't like it, make some more." He cut the onion into large slabs.

"I will, and go easy on that onion." She turned around to the sink and dumped the coffee out of the pot. "God, Curran, as neat as you are, why haven't you ever cleaned this coffee pot?" The old percolator was coated inside with years of built-up coffee grounds.

"You're not supposed to wash them—it spoils the flavor," he said, looking at her as if she were crazy.

"Who told you that?" She picked up a washcloth and began to scrub the pot.

"Somebody . . . Hey! Don't do that!" He grabbed at the pot.

Claire twisted away from his grasp and continued to wash out the muck. "Trust me, Curran!" After cleaning out the pot, she started a fresh batch of coffee.

Curran whipped some eggs in an aluminum bowl, enjoying the company in his kitchen. "Now," he said, dropping the whisk into the sink, "the trick to making a good omelet is making sure the mixture all cooks evenly. . . . You're not watching!" He reached over and nudged her with his foot. "This is my best trick!"

Claire was busy getting dishes out of the cabinet, but she paused to watch him pour the beaten eggs into the hot pan. As soon as the eggs began to set, he placed the cheese, ham, onion, and pepper down on the middle of the omelet. With two quick flicks of the spatula, he covered the filling with the sides of the golden egg mixture.

"I'm impressed!" she said, holding out a plate for him to put it on. He slid the spatula under the omelet. It came easily out of the pan and up onto the serving plate.

"Voilà!" he said proudly, stepping back to admire his work.

"Oh, come on, show-off. Let's eat this thing. You bring the coffee. Let's sit outside." She carried the omelet and plates out to the open deck and set them on the small table. Curran followed, the coffee pot in one hand and two cups in the other.

While she dried off the chairs and sat down, he cut the omelet in two pieces. With a flourish, he placed hers in front of her. Before he could move away, she pulled his face down to hers and kissed him.

"What was that for?" he asked, moving away only slightly.

"Because I'm happy, it's a good morning, and it's been fun." She stared into his eyes as she spoke.

He straightened and picked up the coffee pot. The hot liquid steamed into the cups as she poured. Curran put the pot down and picked up one of the cups, offering it to her.

As she took the cup, he sat down, picked up a

forkful of omelet, and put it in his mouth. "Come on, this is good. Try it," he said, not looking up at her.

She picked up her fork and began to eat. "You're right, it is good."

"So's the coffee. . . . You're right, too." He smiled and took another sip.

The sun had just made its appearance, slowly creeping over the edge of the horizon. Dawn broke over the harbor as they sat on the deck of the houseboat, eating their breakfast. They watched as the fishermen loaded their nets on the boats across the pier.

An insistent beeping noise sounded from the living room. Claire looked over at Curran as he shook his head and stood up. "It's my beeper," he said, walking into the living room. "I'll be back."

She watched as he picked up the beeper, read the message, then turned and punched a number into the phone. He spoke into the receiver and listened, nodding. She stood up and began to pick up the dishes to return them to the kitchen.

"Right, sir, I'll be right there," he said, then hung up the phone.

She was standing in the doorway, holding the plates and the coffee pot, as he turned to face her.

"Back to work? Back after Shaheed and the missiles?" She looked at his silent face and walked past him to the sink.

"So much for our peaceful breakfast." He helped her put the dishes down, then pulled her around to face him. "I have to go."

"I know," she said, staring up into his face. "I

know you have to. If I knew anything more that would help you, I would tell you."

He nodded and kissed her. "Thank you."

She pulled away gently and walked over to her clothes, still piled on the couch were she'd undressed the night before. He watched as she slid the sweatshirt off over her head, drinking in the beauty of her bare body one more time.

She dressed quickly, then turned and walked to the door. "Make damned sure you duck when you're supposed to."

He didn't have time to answer, as she stepped out the door and closed it. He heard the sound of her footsteps as she walked down the deck and jumped off the houseboat onto the dock. "I will," he said to himself, smiling as he walked back into the bedroom to dress.

22

Hawkins, his face puffed and bruised, picked up a sheaf of papers lying next to him on the car seat and stepped out of the GTO, slamming the door behind him. He straightened his uniform, then turned and walked purposefully across the quadrangle and up the steps of the command center.

The room was full of people, all busily staring at computers, talking on phones, and working at the various desks and counters. Monitors on the wall flashed different images and phones jangled incessantly. Curran and an intelligence officer were bent over a table, studying a street map of Beirut. Both men turned as Hawkins walked up.

"Permission to speak with you privately, sir," he said to Curran, saluting as he spoke.

Curran returned the salute. "In my office."

They both turned and walked down the corridor in complete silence. Curran opened the door and held it as Hawkins brushed past. "What is it, Hawk?" he said, closing the door.

A neatly stapled pile of papers flew from Hawkins's hand down on Curran's desk. "I'm transferring out of here. I need your signature."

Curran casually walked around the desk, pulled out his chair, and sat down. He picked up the papers and leafed through them slowly. Cutting his eyes up to Hawkins, he said, "It looks in order to me. Where do I sign?"

Curran's attitude startled Hawkins. He'd expected something else—a lecture, an argument, something, anything more than this quiet acceptance. Hawkins looked down at him, the evidence of last night's fight more than visible on their faces.

"Last page," Hawkins said, continuing to stare at the man behind the desk.

Flipping through the pages again, Curran came to the last page and signed. He picked up the papers and handed them to Hawkins, meeting his stare. Hawkins took the papers and stood there awkwardly, shifting his weight from one foot to the other and struggling for something to say.

The door opened behind him, and Captain Dunne walked over to Curran's desk. Dunne gave each of the men a curious look as he returned their salutes.

"What the hell happened to you two?" he asked, noticing the black eyes, cuts, and abrasions.

"Ran into a door," they both responded at the same time. Hawkins laughed nervously and added, "A big one."

"I see . . ." said Dunne slowly. "Well . . . I came to tell you the balloon's up."

Curran reached over and yanked the papers out of Hawkins's hand, slipping them into his center desk drawer. "Okay, Hawk, let's get to work." His solemn face eased into a smile as his second-in-command grinned and nodded.

Dunne turned and left the room. Hawkins continued to smile, looking at Curran. "Thanks."

"Graham paid a hell of a price for your education. Go draw your gear, get the team together, and meet me in the briefing room." Curran took a key out of his pocket and locked the desk. "NOW!" he said, as he looked up at the man still standing in front of him.

Hawkins pivoted on his heels, swept out the door, and disappeared down the hall. Curran waited until he was gone, then unlocked the drawer and took the papers out. He tore them in half and tossed them into the trash. As he was about to leave, his eyes fell on Graham's copy of Claire's book lying on the desktop. He picked it up and held it, then turned it over to her picture on the back and stared at the image. He placed the book back on the desk, sighed, and gave it a pat.

An hour later, Curran was standing before the team in the briefing room. On the wall behind him was a large map of Lebanon. He was sharing the information he had received earlier from Langley.

". . . And so this is where we're headed. We believe Shaheed is here"—he pointed to an area on the enlargement of the city—"in a ruined tenement house on Rafiq Street. That's right down in the Shi'ite slums of West Beirut."

"Jeezus!" Rexer remarked. "Shitty place to visit." The others muttered in agreement. Hawkins leaned against the wall, watching, but he made no comment.

"This is where all the action is, and intelligence says he's there and the missiles are still with him,"

Curran continued, as Rexer got up and poured himself a paper cup of water.

"Any comments?" he asked.

Rexer turned around and took a sip. "Well, as I recall, that part of Root is full of narrow streets and blind alleys. They've been warring there continuously for over ten years. . . . It looks like hell there."

A laugh rang out from Ramos. "Hey, then it's a good place to look for Shaheed then."

"Yeah," said Leary, playing with a pencil on the table in front of him while he spoke, "it's not a good place for anyone who wants to live, though. Between the Shi'ites, Christians, Druzes, and Palestinians, there are no fewer than eight major warring groups . . . not to mention all the little splinter sects of zealots . . . and all of them shooting at each other."

"Not to mention the Syrian Army that's hosing anything that moves . . . with Soviet armor," added Hawkins, still leaning against the wall.

Although he was usually quiet during the briefings, Dane suddenly spoke up: "What would you say our chances are of reaching target?"

"Assuming we're on our toes, I would say . . . decent," Curran answered.

Rexer wadded up the cup and threw it into a trash can across the room. "What are our chances of getting out?" he asked, slouching down into a chair.

Curran looked around the room slowly. "Marginal."

Ramos whistled. "Jeezus!" The others shifted around, looking at each other.

"Well," said Leary, shaking his head, "that sort of clears the air."

"Anybody want out?" Curran asked.

Ramos turned to Rexer and nudged him. "What do you think?"

Rexer's face could have been made of granite. "I think we're gonna die," he said, looking back at Ramos.

"Not me!" Ramos flashed him a devilish smile. "You know what they say, 'You can't kill a man that was born to hang.' I'm going!"

Curran chuckled, then threw his hands up, signaling the end of the briefing. "Okay, boys, then let's go rumble in the jungle."

The SEALs got up and, one by one, silently exited the room. Hawkins paused for a moment at the door. "This looks bad, Curran."

Curran looked over at him. "We didn't expect him to hide the Stingers in Norfolk, did we? We're walking straight into the eye of the storm. That's why I'm taking only the best with me."

Hawkins smiled. "Thanks. We'll do it."

They left the room together and hurried to a waiting van, into which the other SEALs were throwing equipment bags. After they had loaded up, the van took off to the Naval air base. A jet was waiting for them on the runway, fueled and ready for take-off. After a stop to refuel in the Azores, they headed for an airport in southern Spain. To the wired, restless team, the flight seemed longer than it actually was. It was late evening by the time they touched down.

Another van picked them up just as the jet came to a stop and transported them across the tarmac to a waiting Blackhawk chopper, which took them to the aircraft carrier USS *Ranger*, in the middle of the Mediterranean.

Curran looked down at the luminous dial on his

watch. It was 2400 hours—midnight—as the helicopter touched down on the flight deck. Dunne picked up his briefcase and started off the plane.

"I'll go make sure the chopper is ready while you feed your men. Admiral Grail made special arrangements for you in his private mess."

Being given the battle group admiral's private dining room in which to eat and change into their gear was highly unusual, but Andy Grail was an unusual commander. He was an old-time mariner, a dedicated professional with a special appreciation and affection for the SEALs.

Dunne reached the carrier deck and hurried across the landing area into the control section.

Curran gathered up his maps and motioned to Hawkins. "Get the men and equipment off, and we'll go get some chow. I'll meet you there." Hawkins nodded and turned back to the waiting SEALs. Curran stepped out onto the deck and looked down the length of the carrier. He'd been on them many times, but he was always awed by their size. He walked toward the group of sailors who were waving him over and followed them down to the admiral's galley.

The cooks had left large plates of cold ham and turkey in the middle of a long table, along with some hard rolls, salad, and large pitchers of tea and coffee. All ship's personnel were told to stay clear of the area while the SEALs ate and finished their last-minute briefing. Curran reached across the table and poured himself a cup of coffee.

As he held the cup up to take a sip, his mind flashed to the coffee he'd had on the houseboat. This didn't compare, but at least it was hot and strong.

Setting the cup down, he spread the maps out on

the table. With the maps open and waiting, he walked over and picked up one of the rolls and some turkey. Ramos entered the room first. "Wow, man! Look at this place! I could get my whole family in here for a Sunday meal."

Close behind him were Rexer, Leary, and Dane. They fell on the food like starved dogs on a bone. Leary picked up a roll and threw it to Hawkins as he joined them. He caught it and walked over to Curran. "I think I'll wait until they finish their feeding frenzy. The equipment is stored. By the way, it looks like we've got plenty of time to eat. The chopper not only isn't being readied, the crew hasn't been assembled yet."

"What?" Curran looked at him in disbelief. "We're going to have to use darkness as a cover. It's already half past midnight. What the hell is the hang-up?"

"I don't know, boss. That's just what the guys on deck were telling me." Hawkins poured a cup of coffee and sat down next to Curran.

"Hey!" Rexer held a slab of ham high in the air. "These carrier folks eat real well." He tossed the ham in the air, growled, and snapped it into his mouth.

"Yeah, but they have to live on this tub day in, day out, for months at a time. Not for me, buddy." Leary had made a sandwich, and he walked over to sit down with Curran and Hawkins. "What's up?" he said, as he pulled out a chair, turned it around, and straddled it, facing the two officers.

"Some delaying action. We'll find out when Dunne gets down here." Curran got up and walked over to get some more coffee.

Leary took a bite out of his sandwich and chewed

it slowly, watching Hawkins. "What really happened between you and Curran? You both look like hammered shit."

"I told you. It was raining and slick out there, and Curran and I were walking out to the cars. We slipped and fell."

"Into an empty cement mixer that had been left on . . . right?" Leary gave a knowing smile.

"Something like that," Hawkins answered, his face completely blank. They both looked up as Curran and the others joined them at the table.

"Okay! Listen up now!" Curran bent over the map. "This extract is tricky. We blow the missiles and cross north of the airport to a beach here." He pointed to the spot. "There'll be a sub one mile offshore until dawn." He drew himself up and stood looking at the men around him. "If there are any foul-ups," he continued, "any reason we don't get to the beach before sunrise, we hole up until the following night for pickup. Understood?"

"In other words," droned Dane, "we're fucked puppies if we miss the bus."

"Exactly." Curran looked down at his watch. They had been on the carrier for over an hour, and he was growing impatient. Looking down at Hawkins, he asked, "Where the hell is Dunne?"

Hawkins shrugged his shoulders. As the team finished eating, they walked around the room, looking at the admiral's Spartan but well laid-out facility. Dane stretched out on one of the tables and tried to sleep. Rexer, Ramos, and Leary sat down near the door and played cards with a deck Ramos had stashed in his pocket.

Hawkins rose from the table. "I'll go get our uniforms. We can at least get dressed." He tagged Dane on the way out. Dane got up and followed him.

After a few minutes, Captain Dunne walked in. A look of frustration clouded his face as he approached Curran. "Still no go."

Curran slammed his fist on the table. "What the shit are they hung on?"

"I think it's called red tape," Dunne said, "or, in the vernacular, bureaucratic bullshit."

"But we got the go-ahead from Stinson. I don't understand." Curran began to pace, realized what he was doing, and sat down.

The door to the passageway swung open, and Dane and Hawkins walked in carrying two large canvas bags containing their clothes and weapons. The card players stopped and walked over, anxious to get started.

"Look at this!" exclaimed Ramos, pulling the clothes from the bag. "Syrian Army fatigues."

Dane unzipped the canvas sack containing the weapons. "Oh, shit! AK47s! This is not my weapon of choice," he complained to Hawkins.

"Yeah," Hawkins responded, "but it happens to be what the Syrians use. Think *covert*—got it? God, you'll carry your own weapon, of course."

Dane happily picked up a set of fatigues and threw them over the table to Curran.

"I think I'll get some coffee." Dunne stood up and walked over to the serving table as Curran scrambled into his new clothing.

After everyone was dressed in the Syrian uniforms, the anxiety of the wait began to set in. Dunne took his cup of coffee and leaned against the wall, watching the SEAL team as they began to move around the room nervously. They were strung tight. The waiting was the hardest part of any mission. Dunne knew that once a commitment was made, the waiting became a physical pain.

It was ten minutes before two o'clock when a young ensign ran into the room. He stopped dead in his tracks, startled by the group of men in foreign uniforms. "Uh, uh—I'm looking for Captain Dunne," he finally stuttered out.

"Over here!" Dunne said, from the end of the table. He got up and walked over to meet the ensign.

The young officer continued to stare at the strangely clad men standing around him menacingly as he handed Dunne a piece of paper. "This came for you, sir."

Dunne snatched the paper out of his hand and read it. "Well, Washington finally figured out how many people have to sign off on this thing. We're on green light!"

There were loud whoops and applause from the SEALs.

"We're already two hours behind!" Curran grumbled.

Dunne turned to him. "If you're not comfortable with the time, you have full authority to abort."

"NO WAY!" Rexer yelled, followed by Ramos, who yelled out loudly, jarring the young ensign who was still standing there. "Pussies exit left!"

Curran shot a steely look at Dunne. "I think we're ready." Turning to his men, he yelled, "Let's go do it!"

The ensign snapped a salute to Dunne and hurriedly made his exit, knocking over a chair in his rush to the door. The men picked up their weapons and took off down the passageway.

They emerged to the sound of whining helicopter turbines. The waiting CH-47 was ready. The last bit of their equipment had been tossed on board. The men ran across the deck, buffeted by the strong gusts of wind from the rotors, and climbed in.

Dunne grabbed Curran's hand and shook it as the SEAL commander started out to the chopper. Curran nodded and climbed aboard. The deck lights blazed brightly across the mammoth deck of the aircraft carrier. A flight-deck crewman, from his position on the runway, raised his hands, and the chopper lifted up off the deck, whirling upward into the night sky.

In the operations tower, the ensign who had given the message to Dunne was standing next to a young crewman. Along with all the other personnel in the tower, they watched as the chopper lifted off.

"What's going on out there, sir?" the bewildered crewman asked, having watched the strangely clad men as they boarded the chopper.

"I'm not at all sure. . . . But that's the spookiest bunch I've ever seen!" the ensign replied, obviously shaken after his encounter with the group. "I don't know who they're going after, but whoever it is, he's in trouble."

The lights from the aircraft carrier soon disappeared below them. The chopper climbed high and fast into the sky and set a straight course for the Persian Gulf.

23

Curran settled back against the big ribs of the aircraft and closed his eyes. He worked the plan over and over in his mind, reviewing each detail and remembering that all good plans are fluid because many changes could and would occur after the mission began.

The best weapons Curran had in his arsenal were his men. Their training and coolness under fire would be tested again and again in the coming hours. But his confidence was jarred when he thought about Hawkins.

According to the rules, he should have fired him after the last mission. Failing that, he should have accepted his transfer papers. He knew Hawkins was the weakest link in his chain, but, somehow, he also knew Hawkins had all the right stuff. He could be a great SEAL commander if he had learned his lesson when Graham died. Curran felt sure he had. . . . But now he began to question that judgment. He was betting the success of this mission, his life, and the lives of his entire team on the hope that Hawkins would perform.

The chopper began to descend rapidly to the drop-off point. Curran instructed Rexer and Ramos to inflate the Zodiac. They jerked up the rubber boat and hit the valves. The boat popped into shape, and the two men started moving it to the open ramp in the back.

Bracing themselves against the sides of the chopper, the team moved up to the edge of the ramp. The chopper was skimming the top of the water as the crew chief motioned to Curran. The Zodiac slid off the ramp, and the men dove into the ocean behind it.

24

The Zodiac bobbed on the waves as the six men climbed in. When everyone was on board, Ramos flicked on the little engine and they sped quietly toward the shore. Curran was nervous. The contact man they'd arranged for onshore had been expecting them two hours earlier. Without him, they would be looking for the proverbial needle in a haystack—an intensely hostile haystack.

Beirut held horror and grim remembrances for every SEAL in the Zodiac; they had all been there before. It was a place to which none of them would ever have chosen to return. Now, they stared at Beirut's nearing skyline with awe and apprehension. The town perched on the coast like a starved, impatient vulture.

The city's outline was occasionally lit by flashes from RPG hits and artillery. As they reached the shore, they could hear the rattle of small-arms fire from different parts of the city blend into one low, continuous hum. It was a murmur of death.

Leary nudged Rexer as the Zodiac brought them up to the rocks. "You believe that shit?" he said, looking at the hellscape in front of them.

Rexer whispered, "Warning . . . trespassers will be shot. Survivors will be shot again."

Signaling for their attention, Curran whispered hoarsely, "Remember, the extract point is one mile offshore. The sub will be there until dawn. The minute the sun scrapes the water, it'll be outta here—for good."

The Zodiac came to a stop on the rocky edge of the beach. Dane jumped over and balanced on the rocks. He held the craft as the others leaped out to join him. They stood warily on the stony promontory as Dane deflated the Zodiac and turned toward them. "There goes our return ticket," he said, as the rubber craft shriveled and floated away.

Hawkins grabbed Curran's arm and muttered, "Are you sure we're in the right place?"

"Yes." Curran peered desperately through the darkness for the contact who was supposed to meet them here.

"Where's our man?" Leary asked, as the two team leaders came up to where he was waiting.

"We're late. He's probably skyed by now. Let's move out." Curran motioned the team forward. They began to wrap their khaki Bedouin Kaffiyeh scarves around their heads and move up the beach, their weapons held in readiness.

As they started to move, they heard a loud scrape. The flame of a match illuminated the face of a person sitting in an abandoned car a few feet ahead of them. The impassive face belonged to a boy in his early teens. He beckoned them forward and waited calmly as they approached. He held an AK47 across his legs and stared at them through coal-black eyes.

"You from Amal?" Curran asked, crouching down beside the boy.

The kid looked at him and nodded. "Ali," he said, and got out of the car. He walked up the beach, not speaking another word. The team fell in behind him and moved quietly across the sand.

Ali led them down the Corniche waterfront promenade, which had been heavily damaged by artilleryfire. They passed a sign with an international "No Tanks" symbol. The sign was barely legible, having been blasted with what appeared to be shotgun pellets. Every pile of rubble and trash, every creak of the boards under their feet, increased the tension.

Dane stepped over to an unoccupied Land Rover that looked to be in good shape. "Let's ride! I can get this thing started."

Curran waved his hand, beckoning him back. "Cars get stopped. It's safer to walk."

Hawkins stumbled over the rotting carcass of a dog. He looked down in revulsion. "Jezzus!" he said under his breath to Curran. "This cesspool of a place is some kind of weird."

With Ali out in front, they left the beach and filed through a vast warren of crumbling, burned-out wreckage that had once been a row of modern, highrise buildings. Twisted pieces of steel emerged from the blown-up concrete like huge claws scratching at the sky.

"The dark side of the moon," Rexer whispered, staring in awe at the ruins.

223

Leary turned around to Hawkins. "Where in hell are we?" he asked, as they began to slow down.

Hawkins watched the shadows as a cloud passed over. "This is the Green Line," he said. "Dividing line between east and west Beirut. We are where the action is."

Continuous, sporadic gunfire crackled in the distance. Ali stopped and pointed out the different sources of the firing.

"Phalange . . . Druze . . . Palestinian . . . Syrian . . . Amal . . . Hisbollah . . . Al Shuhada . . ." the boy said, indicating the various hostiles in the area. He looked up and pointed to the lights of a jet crossing the mountains on the far side of the horizon. "Israeli." Ali stopped his recitation and continued walking through the chunks of the concrete and steel hulk of the bombed buildings. The team stayed close on his heels.

As they crossed the Green Line, they entered an area in which the buildings were only partially bombed. Ali motioned for them to follow as he slipped inside one of them.

Entering, Ramos switched on his small flashlight and bounced the beam against a stack of brand-new Sony VCRs, still in the manufacturer's crates. "What is this shit?"

Suddenly the beam hit four Arab gunmen huddled between the crates of VCRs. The room exploded in frenzied gunfire, and silenced bursts strobed in the darkness with uncanny accuracy. The firing stopped as suddenly as it started. The boy stood still, frozen in shock.

Ramos flashed the beam around the room again.

All four of the Arabs were lying motionless on the ground. Ali looked back at the SEALs approvingly.

"Anybody hit?" Curran called out quietly.

Rexer looked around. "We're good!" he answered, as he began to rifle the bodies, kicking away their guns. Hawkins picked up a bullet-riddled knapsack and watched as white powder began to pour out of the holes.

"Christ! It's cocaine. They're smugglers!" he said in amazement.

"Druze," Ali said, looking at the men lying around the room.

One of the gunmen opened his eyes and watched the Americans draw nearer. As Rexer leaned over him, he sprang up, aiming his Makarov pistol at the big SEAL's chest. Hawkins moved like lightning, dropping the man before he could fire with a quick burst from his AK. Rexer again leaned forward and ripped the Makarov out of the dead Druze's hand.

"Shitty little gun for a shitty little man," he said, tossing the weapon across the room.

Ali started out of the building. Curran signaled for the others to move out. They traveled down narrow, littered paths that only ten years before had been wide modern avenues. That time was impossible to imagine now as they crept hurriedly between mounds of crushed glass, rusting steel, and broken concrete.

Rising all around them were the silent, forbidding shells of buildings. They climbed over a large pile of steel that blocked their way, discovering as they scuttled over that it had once been a large tourist bus. The area they were traveling through was appropriately named the Devil's Playground. The men wondered if even the devil would want to play there.

The concrete around them suddenly exploded, as a rifle fired from above. Everyone scattered, diving behind broken car bodies and piles of trash. Curran crawled over to Dane, who was hiding behind some twisted steel. He motioned for the man to lean over. As Dane bent forward, Curran whispered hoarsely, "See if you can work your way to high ground and give us some cover." Dane nodded, then slipped down over the steel and out into the darkness.

As he continued to crawl through the wreckage, Curran tapped Hawkins on the leg and motioned for him to follow. The bullets fired from overhead pinged wildly around them as they moved toward the others. Curran's voice hissed out instructions: "Hawkins and I will move fifty yards to the right to draw fire. The rest of you hold position and fire when ordered." He looked at Hawkins. "Ready?" Hawkins nodded.

The two men sprinted across the street, their bodies hunched over their weapons. They found cover behind a shattered wall and stopped.

Dane watched them from his perch on another broken wall. Carefully bracing against the remains of a windowsill, he readied his rifle. He pulled his mouthpiece forward and spoke into it. "Bad Karma, this is God. I'm in position about a hundred meters to the left of your position. I'm—"

A Druze gunman sprang out from the darkness behind him, firing his AK. As the slugs ripped into his back, Dane spun around and fired the round in his rifle. The Arab dropped and rolled over on his

226

back. Dane staggered to regain his balance then fell over in a heap.

"God, this is Bad Karma. . . ." Curran heard the broken transmission and the sounds of the quick struggle on the wall. He spoke into the headset. "Come in, God." There was no answer. Curran turned to Hawkins, who had also been listening. "Stay put," he said hurriedly. "I'm going to check Dane out."

Picking through the rubble, Curran worked his way up the hill of crushed brick toward Dane's position. The quiet was unnatural, making every jostled brick that fell sound like a crashing boulder.

He scrambled over a wall that abruptly shifted forward under his weight and collapsed. Curran fought to catch his footing as everything crumbled and broke loose beneath him. He tumbled and slid down through the bricks, concrete, and glass, then rolled to a stop at the foot of a clearing. Hearing a noise behind him, Curran pulled himself up and spun around.

Two bearded men had stepped around a wall and watched as he fell through the rubble. They both carried AKs, and the weapons were pointed directly at him. The older of the two moved toward him, barking a question in Arabic, while the younger man stood back, looking around for any other Syrians.

Curran lowered his head and spoke into the mouthpiece, "Race Riot, this is Bad Karma. I've got company."

The younger guard blinked his eyes in amazement when he heard the man speaking. "You are American?" Curran could tell by the tone that the young Druze starting toward him wasn't going to shake his hand.

"God . . . God . . ." Curran called into the mouthpiece.

The young Arab had a twisted smile on his face as he swaggered up to Curran. "American asshole," he said as he stuck his weapon into Curran's face. "Your god doesn't help you now!"

A bullet hit the top of the young Druze's skull, sending blood, tissue, and bone fragments flying into the air. The older Druze dropped next as a second round came over the wall and hit him in the back of the neck, shattering his spinal cord and exiting through his throat. The impact threw him forward, knocking him over onto Curran.

Over the headset Curran had heard Dane breathing, a deep, labored rattle, as he gasped out each word: "All yuppies must die!"

Curran looked up and watched as Dane swayed on the edge of the wall above him. Blood covered the front of his shirt and ran out the side of his mouth. He looked down at Curran as he teetered on the edge of the burned building.

Making one last great effort, Dane threw his arms up toward the sky, his rifle extended over his head in a victory gesture. Then his body seemed to collapse from the knees upward as he dropped the gun and toppled headlong off the wall.

Hawkins was waiting as Curran scurried over the rubble toward him, carrying Dane's rifle. "God?"

"He's dead," Curran answered, his voice flat and hard. Swinging his arm over his head, he motioned for Ali and the others to move out. He slung Dane's

228

specialized sniper rifle over his chest as he hurried to catch up with Ali.

Curran pulled Ramos over. "Tell Ali we need to hurry, we need to move faster. It's getting close to daylight."

Ramos rattled a fast phrase to the boy, who nodded an acknowledgment and began to run down the narrow, shabby streets toward the sounds of artillery bombardments and gunfire. The five SEALs ran with him, rushing down through the corridors of hell. Curran said nothing to Rexer, Leary, or Ramos about Dane's death, but they saw the rifle bouncing across his back as they raced down the street and knew Dane was gone.

The first blue hints of the approaching dawn began to slip across the edges of the horizon as the SEALs made their way into the Shi'ite slums of West Beirut. Ragged laundry was strung on clotheslines outside the windows of the dilapidated, destroyed buildings, and pictures of the Ayatollah Khomeini were plastered on every remaining wall.

Ali stopped running and paused by one of the walls. "Here"—he made a sweeping movement with his hand—"Al Shuhada."

Ramos looked around at the large posters of the scowling old Iranian ayatollah. "I think this neighborhood qualifies for an urban eradication program."

Curran whipped around to Hawkins. "Time?" he asked.

Looking down at the black watch strapped to his wrist, Hawkins responded, "Forty-two minutes."

"Shit!" Curran gasped. "We're an hour behind. We've got to hustle!"

They began to pick up the pace, slipping through the last of the night's shadows. Ali stopped abruptly and Curran, who was right behind him, held up his fist. Everyone stopped and dropped down into a crouched position, their weapons pointed in the direction in which Curran and Ali were staring.

The Al Shuhada had a checkpoint set up on the street in front of them. Six Arab gunmen were stationed on either side of the narrow street, forming an effective block for anyone who might wander up.

Ali signaled for the SEALs to move over to where he stood on the right, near the entry to a small alley. They moved quietly down the narrow passage, one behind the other. Twenty meters down the alley was a drain, cutting up under the pavement. Ali dropped down into the culvert, motioning for the others to follow.

The culvert was a sewage ditch that had been there for decades. A thick coating of raw sewage clung to the walls. The smell gagged them as they crawled along the dark, stinking culvert behind Ali. Ahead, they could see a dim ray of light coming through a hole overhead. Ali found a handhold on the wall and pulled himself up and out, then stuck his hand down to the others, helping them out of the sewer.

They came up on a street at the base of a hill, well past the checkpoint. Ali grabbed Curran's arm and pointed to a multistoried white stone building at the top of the hill. "There," he said.

Curran started up the hill, then stopped, aware that Ali was standing motionless by the culvert. He turned and looked back at the boy. Ali stood still, not making any effort to join them. "I go," he said. Curran turned and walked down to him.

"Thanks," Curran said, holding his hand out to the boy. Ali stared at it with his dead eyes, then turned on his heels and walked off slowly into the night without another word.

Time was running out, and Curran didn't have the luxury to try to figure the kid out. Turning, he joined the others, who were waiting for him. He beckoned them over into the shelter of a small enclave.

"Okay," he whispered hoarsely, "the Stingers are in the basement of that building. Amal said there were only two guards there, because the place is guarded by checkpoints set up all around this hill, like the one we just saw. Rexer, you, Ramos, and Hawkins will enter through the side window, set the charges in the building, and exit through the front. Leary and I will cover the building. Let's go!"

Darting from one pile of cover to another, they worked their way up the hill to some shadowy rubble.

"That's it!" Curran whispered to Hawkins. "Time?"

Hawkins shook his head. "Twenty minutes."

"We'd better get this done fast or we're gonna miss our sub!" said Curran, as they all converged on the darkened building.

Hawkins, Ramos, and Rexer went around the left side of the building, while Leary and Curran crept around the building from the right, checking for the guards. Leary stayed close to the building, while Curran ranged out farther.

As Leary eased around the side of the darkened

231

building to the front, an Al Shuhada guard emerged from the doorway. The man's rifle was slung over his shoulder. He stepped out the door, looking from side to side. He yawned and stretched, then walked back in.

Leary spoke into the mike on his headset: "I see him, boss, and I can hear him and his buddy in the room next to the door. I'll take care of it." He slid around the corner and disappeared into the doorway.

Curran worked his way around through the piles of debris and crawled to the top of a pile across from the main entrance to the building. He pulled Dane's sniper rifle around, looking through the starlight scope first, and then through the thermal. He heard Leary's transmission and saw the guard walk back into the building. Leary was about twenty steps behind him.

The images through the thermal were all cool greens and blues, indicating no heat sources or living creatures around the building. He saw a flash of red as he swung the thermal back around to the door, and he switched back to the starlight. It was Leary coming out the front door. "Done!" was Leary's brief report into the mike as he scurried through the wreckage toward Curran.

"No problems?" asked Curran, as Leary dropped down beside him.

"Nope. There were two, now there are none. That's a weird building, boss."

"How's that?" Curran asked, as he continued to sweep the area, looking through the scope.

"Must be a training facility. There are a lot of rooms with books and blackboards in them," Leary answered, jamming another of the curved ammo clips into his weapon.

Before Curran could comment, Hawkins stepped out, then held the door open as Ramos and Rexer stood by the opening. Rexer stepped out and planted another charge by the door, carefully setting the radio receiver that would set off the charges. The others kept watch. As soon as he had finished he waved up to Curran and they all scattered out into the rubble, running for cover.

Hawkins reached the rubble heap first. He was all smiles as he handed Curran the radio detonator. "Bingo, boss. They were all there . . . all four of 'em, and Rexer has all the charges set. Let's blow and go."

Curran nodded and slapped him on the back. "Okay! Now let's—"

He was interrupted by Leary grabbing his arm. "No! Look!" he said, pointing frantically toward the building.

Hawkins and Curran snapped their heads around in the direction in which Leary was pointing and their faces fell. Six children, accompanied by two women, appeared on the sidewalk in front of the building. They were singing and giggling as they walked up the street.

The men watched with horror as the children turned and entered through the door Hawkins had left standing open. At the far end of the street they could see more children heading up in the same direction.

"Those bastards planted the missiles in a school!" Curran said, not believing what he was seeing through the eerie half-light of dawn.

"We've got to blow it. NOW!" Hawkins whispered urgently.

"NO!" Curran shook his head emphatically. "We can't! Maybe they'll see the bodies of the guards and get the hell out."

"No they won't," Leary answered. "I shoved them in a closet and closed the door."

Farther down the street, they could see other groups of children as them made their way to the school. There were a few unarmed adults, probably teachers, leading the kids up the street.

"The longer we wait, the more kids will go in that building! This is our last chance!" Hawkins said, pleading with Curran.

There was a pause, then Curran turned and handed him the detonator, throwing Dane's rifle to Ramos. "I'm going in to flush those kids. If I'm not out in five minutes," he said, leveling his eyes at Hawkins, "blow it."

Hawkins looked down at the detonator in his hand. "Why me?" he said, looking back up at Curran.

Curran forced a smile. "You're the only one trigger-happy enough to hit the switch when I'm in the building." He stared at Hawkins for a second. "Understood?"

Hawkins took a deep breath and nodded. Giving him a slap on the arm, Curran plunged around the rubble and disappeared behind a half-standing wall.

Dashing from one shadowy hole to another, he reached the front of the school. Reaching inside his trouser pocket, he pulled out a smoke grenade and held it tightly in his hand as he rushed into the building. The lights were still off in the darkened

234

classrooms on the first floor as he ran down the hall. At the base of the stairs he stopped and looked up, hearing voices coming from the second floor.

Curran took the stairs three at a time, racing up the staircase. Happy, excited chatter came from one of the rooms on the left side of the hall.

As he lunged into the room, he saw one of the women and four of the children over near the windows. The woman threw her hands out over the children, and they all dropped to the ground. "No!" Curran shouted, grabbing the woman by the arm and yanking her up from the floor. "Get out of here! Get them out!" He pushed her toward the door and started pulling the children up and shoving them toward her. The woman looked at him, but then a glimmer of understanding crossed her face and she began to herd the children toward the door.

They scrambled out into the hallway and started for the stairs as the other teacher looked into the hallway to see what was happening. She screamed and ran back into the room. Curran turned on his heels and ran into the room behind her. The woman hovered in a corner, wailing loudly in Arabic, as the other two children clung to her, crying. He yelled and motioned for her to move, but she continued to stand there, her arms around the children.

"Oh, God, lady!" Curran screamed at her. "Get out of here!" He pulled the pin on the grenade and threw it to the far corner of the room. The grenade made a loud popping noise and smoke began to billow though the room. Curran pulled the woman from the corner. She screamed loudly as she broke away from him and ran for the door, leaving the children behind. They stared at him, frozen with fear. Curran slung his rifle over his shoulder and grabbed the kids. They were like deadweight in his arms, seemingly resigned to whatever fate awaited them. He turned and dashed out of the room, holding the children in his arms as he ran.

The others had already cleared the building. He stumbled down the stairs holding tightly to the little ones. He could hear screams outside as the children and teachers ran down the street, away from the building. Curran dashed down the hallway and out through the front door.

The children in his arms came out of their initial shock and started yelling and kicking. He stopped just outside the entry and turned them loose. They went flying down the street to join the others as he reached up to unsling his rifle. Scanning the street, he saw two gunmen on the balcony of a building across from him. They had both spotted him and were swinging their weapons around toward the school.

One of the gunmen on the balcony was Ben Shaheed. He had Curran in his sights and squeezed the trigger, firing several bullets before Curran could take aim.

The bullets slammed into Curran, causing him to spin around and fall to the ground in front of the doorway. Ramos fired a round with the sniper rifle, dropping one of the men on the balcony. The other man dove through an open window. Leary cut loose with a barrage of fire at the balcony.

The gunfire stopped as abruptly as it had started. Hawkins gripped the detonator tightly as they looked back at the school.

"I think he's wasted," Ramos said, his voice dull

and hollow as he stared at the crumpled body of Curran lying on the ground.

"I don't think so!" Hawkins shook his head, not wanting to believe it.

As they watched, the form on the ground gave a jerk and struggled to turn sideways.

"Look!" Hawkins shouted. "He's alive!"

Curran slowly raised his fist toward them. They watched as he moved his hand up and down.

"Damn you, Curran!" Hawkins muttered under his breath.

Ramos stared in disbelief as he said quietly, "He wants you to detonate."

Hawkins turned and placed the detonator into Ramos's hand. "Fuck him! I'm not going to blow him up and make him a hero. Take this." He jammed a new clip into his AK, dropped into a sprint position, and took off.

Blasting away at the buildings surrounding the school, Hawkins dashed madly down the street. Tracer bullets sprayed up around him as he dodged and darted toward the fallen Curran. Ramos, Leary, and Rexer raked the building with cover fire as Hawkins fell down flat next to Curran.

"You dumb ass. You dumb fuck!" he said to Curran as he panted, gasping for air.

Curran rolled over and looked at him. "Go on . . . get out of here," he said feebly.

"No way, hero. We're leaving this shithole together!" Hawkins yanked Curran up on his shoulders and began to zigzag back up the block.

Two more gunmen appeared, firing wildly from the upper-floor windows of a tenement on the street ahead of them. Bullets hit the pavement around

Hawkins's feet and pinged against walls as he ducked into a doorway for cover.

"Blow it, Ramos!" he shouted into his mouthpiece. "Blow it!"

Ramos pressed the fire button on the M122 demolition firing device as he, Leary, and Rexer dropped down into a tight crouch behind the wall. The loud thunderclap of the explosion rolled across the Shi'ite slums as the school building turned into yet another pile of Beirut rubble.

On the heels of the first blast came another sharp crack as the warheads and rocket mortars of the Stingers exploded.

Some of the buildings near the school, unstable from earlier artillery bombardments and bombings, fell apart. Their walls crumbled and smashed forward into the streets below. Fire and debris fell like the rains of hell on the blackened, battle-scorched buildings.

25

Captain Dunne looked anxiously through the periscope of the USS *Denver*. He could clearly see the skyline of Beirut boldly silhouetted on the horizon across the morning sky. Nothing moved across the water but seagulls swooping and diving through the waves. Dunne sighed and turned the scope over to the seaman standing next to him.

The interior of the observation deck was tight. Dunne turned around and stood beside the submarine's captain. The submariner was looking over a computer readout as Dunne brushed against him. He glanced up at the SEAL commandant, then back to the paper in his hand. His face was tired and grim.

"Look, Dunne, I've got a billion-dollar piece of machinery here. If I hazard this ship and disobey orders, then I'm looking at a court-martial."

"Ten more minutes! That's all I'm asking," Dunne said, his own face showing his frustration and tension.

"You've been doing this to me for the last hour, in twenty-minute increments. I can't do it any more!" The captain put his hand on Dunne's shoulder, then turned to his first mate. "Let's change neighborhoods."

Dunne shrugged the man's hand off and looked away. "Damn it!" he said disgustedly, knowing that the submariner had no other choice.

"We'll cruise in a circle for the next hour, but then . . . we've got to go," the captain said grudgingly. His tone expressed his sympathy for Dunne's situation.

The explosion knocked Hawkins off his feet, and he fell forward into the doorway. Curran flopped motionlessly on top of him. Hawkins rolled over and pushed Curran around so he could see his face. "Hey, don't flake out on me now."

Curran's eyelids fluttered, and a smile formed on his lips. "Stingers?"

"Blown to hell," Hawkins said, as he pulled himself up to a kneeling position and looked up the street in the direction of the three SEALs rushing toward them.

Rexer and Leary ducked into the doorway, joining Hawkins and Curran, as Ramos darted across the street and crouched down behind a burned-out car body. Leary knelt down beside Curran and began to rip away the blood-soaked Syrian fatigues. Cradling Curran's head on his knees, Hawkins winced as he looked at the holes in Curran's body. Reaching around into his pack, Leary hurriedly applied emergency dressings to the open, bleeding wounds. Curran was losing consciousness, and he moaned softly as the medic worked on him.

"How bad?"

Leary flipped a quick look at Hawkins. "We got an abdominal and we got a hip. Losing some serious blood."

There were loud shouts from up the street as several Al Shuhada gunmen rushed toward them, firing steadily as they ran.

"We got to get out of here!" Ramos yelled from across the street.

Hawkins nodded. "Let's move it out, now. Leary, you carry Curran."

"I got him." Leary reached down and pulled Curran up on his back. Rexer jumped out into the street, his assault rifle blazing, as Leary dashed across the street with Curran dangling over his back and took cover with Ramos behind the car. Rexer and Hawkins darted down the street and fired from an alleyway as Ramos opened up over the top of a burned-out fender, firing while the medic darted down to the others.

One Arab gunman jumped from a doorway and opened fire on Leary as he ran to the alley. Ramos fired three rapid bursts into the man, dropping him. Then he ran backward, firing as he went, down to where the others waited.

Five more armed figures moved furtively from the rubble and doorways around the SEALs in the alley. Rexer looked around frantically for more suitable cover, then grabbed Hawkins to get his attention. "Look!" He motioned to the remains of a wall less than fifty yards behind them.

"That's better than this!" Hawkins replied, motioning for the others to follow as he and Rexer sprinted backward and dove behind the wall. They rolled up on their feet and provided covering fire as the others fell over the wall after them.

Rexer jammed a curved clip into his AK. "Damn! This is a downright unfriendly bunch of assholes!"

The Al Shuhadas broke from cover and rushed toward the alleyway. The four SEALs met them with a hail of fire. Falling back, the Arabs took cover and stopped firing. The street grew quiet again.

Nearby, a car engine roared to life and the sound of a horn began to blare in the stillness. Hawkins looked over at Curran and watched the man's chest rise and fall rhythmically. He was still breathing. Suddenly, Rexer tugged at his sleeve and pointed up the street.

A new red Mercedes 500SE was roaring toward them, lights flashing, horn honking, and a white flag whipping from the antenna.

"What the fuck is that!" Rexer asked, as the vehicle came to a stop in front of them. They all watched with amazement as the doors opened and two middle-aged Al Shuhada elders in slacks and T-shirts got out of the car, holding their hands over their heads. The men stood by the car for a moment, then started walking cautiously toward them, broad smiles across their faces.

One of the men shouted out to them in perfect English. "Please! Let us stop the killing."

Without a word, all four SEALs raised their guns and fired, killing both of the men instantly. As the Arabs fell forward, the pistols tucked into the backs of their belts came into view.

Hawkins motioned toward the Mercedes. "Let's

go!'' They all piled into the car and pulled out into the street, Rexer driving. Hawkins reached out the window and yanked the white flag off the antenna. He turned to Rexer as he threw it on the floor. "People get hosed in this town for pretending to be what they're not."

The remaining Al Shuhada men hesitated before firing on the car. The hesitation was all the time Rexer needed to back the car out of the alley.

Roaring down the street toward the Al Shuhada position, the SEALs leaned out the windows and fired. The startled Arabs dove for cover as the Mercedes smashed past them.

Ben Shaheed's black eyes flashed with rage as the car plunged through the wreckage and up the street. He raised his rifle over his head and waved it madly, yelling in Arabic for his fighters to follow the Mercedes.

He and six of his men jumped into a blue Ford van parked at the curb. The driver gunned the van to life and spun the wheels as the van screeched off the curb and down the street after the escaping Mercedes.

In the back seat, Curran groaned. Hawkins looked over his shoulder. "Just hang on, boss. We're going to take a little ride." Suddenly a turbaned gunman stepped out from a smashed storefront and aimed his rifle at the car. Ramos fired rapidly from the back seat, and the man fell back into the store.

"Anybody got extra mags? I'm getting a little short here!" Ramos yelled.

"Pocket . . . pocket!" Curran gasped.

"Thanks, boss!" Ramos said, as he pulled the extra magazines from the wounded man's trouser pouch. He pushed a loaded magazine in and leaned back out the window. They were forced to slow down and thread their way carefully around burned-out automobiles, over piles of concrete, and around huge rocket craters in the road.

They no longer had the darkness to cover them. It was morning. The sun was rising over the worn-out city of Beirut.

As the Mercedes pulled up over a rise, the coast came into view off to their left. Hawkins pointed and yelled to Rexer, "That way! Back toward the ocean!"

Rexer swung the car around and gunned the engine, heading back down toward the ocean. The street was a maze of twists and turns. Large stacks of concrete and debris made their progress difficult. As they pulled around a corner, Ramos grabbed Hawkins and yelled, "Shit! It's another roadblock!"

Facing them at the end of the street was an armored personnel carrier, mounted with a .50-caliber machine gun. Several armed Al Shuhada fighters were positioned around it.

Rexer swung the wheel and threw the Mercedes into a 180-degree slide, then roared away in the opposite direction. The surprised gunmen opened fire on the retreating car.

Bullets ripped into the windshield, scattering glass fragments over everyone. Rexer's head jerked forward. One of the Arab bullets had caught him at the base of his skull.

The Mercedes swerved crazily off the road and flipped over, sliding upside down into the side of a gutted building.

Choking and spitting dust, Leary crawled from the

wreckage and reached back in to check on Rexer. Hawkins wiped the broken glass from his face with his sleeve and looked over at Leary as he rolled out of the wrecked Mercedes, pulling Curran out of the back seat as he emerged. "Well?"

"Rexer's dead."

Ramos groaned. "I got a problem here." Both Hawkins and Leary turned around and looked into the wreckage. One of Ramos's legs was pinned underneath the edge of the car door.

Leary dropped down beside him. "Hey, Ramos. No sweat, buddy! I can get you out." He and Hawkins clawed away the rubble around the little Cuban's leg and eased the limb out from the door.

Hawkins's face was cut and bloody, but otherwise he was all right. He noticed that Leary appeared to be hit in the upper arm. He watched the medic help Ramos up. "You okay?" he asked Leary, looking at the bullet hole in his sleeve.

"Flesh wound—I'm good to go," he said, supporting Ramos's weight as they both stood.

Ramos put his damaged leg on the ground and shifted his weight onto it. "Ohhh, it smarts, but it's not broken! I can make it."

Hawkins looked over at Curran, who was still breathing but unconscious. He lifted him up and threw him over his shoulder like a rag doll. "Okay, let's get to the ocean." They began to weave their way between the buildings and down the hill to the water. There was still a large garbage dump to be crossed; it lay between them and the beach.

Ben Shaheed's driver had been unable to keep up with the Mercedes as it plowed through the streets. The man was trembling as he pulled to a stop next to the wrecked Mercedes. Shaheed swung the door open and watched two of his men scramble down the slope to the wreck.

"There's only one here! He's dead," one of the men shouted back to Shaheed. The Arab's dark eyes immediately searched the surrounding area. He hit the side of the door with his fist as he spotted the disappearing figures by the garbage dump. Cursing, he called his men back to the car, then slammed the door and barked an order to his driver.

As Hawkins climbed over the last pile of garbage, he came to a low clay cliff that dropped down to the beach. He warily started down the slope, lost his footing in some loose sand, and began to slide. It was the easy way down, he thought to himself, as he and Curran landed in the sand. Hawkins lay next to the wounded man, catching his breath.

As Hawkins gasped for air, he looked out toward the water. It was as if he were in another world. Snow-white sand stretched out to an iridescent blue-green ocean. The only sounds he could hear were the surf and the calls of seagulls.

Ramos and Leary crashed onto the sand next to him.

"Man," Ramos said, trying to catch his breath, "it's been one helluva day!"

"Yep," Hawkins said, as he stood up and picked up Curran. "And we need to go see if our bus really did leave without us. I don't like it here at Camp Runamucka." He threw Curran up on his back and trudged down to the water's edge.

Placing Curran on the sand next to him, he reached around into his pack for his swim fins.

Leary and Ramos were already in theirs, waiting for him, as he stood up again.

"You're not dragging me out there," Curran said weakly.

"Well, good mornin', darlin'!" Hawkins responded. "Let's put your little swim shoes on, since you're awake." He reached into Curran's pack and pulled out his fins.

"No!" Curran tried to pull his feet away but couldn't. Hawkins slipped the fins onto Curran's feet.

"Hey, look now. It's either die here on the beach or in the water. We might as well make those assholes work!" He bent over to pick up Curran.

"Leave me. I'm deadweight."

"Forget it."

"That's an order."

Hawkins threw his head back and laughed. "You're delirious, son. You're no longer in charge here."

Curran's hand suddenly shot forward and snatched Hawkins's Kalishnikov. He held the rifle steady, aiming it directly into Hawkins's face. Hawkins slowly straightened up as he stared down the rifle barrel. Ramos and Leary moved closer. Hawkins waved them away.

"You're not going to save all those Lebanese kids and then kill me.... Not all in the same day." Hawkins smiled and watched as Curran fought to hold the gun steady. "I probably could sleep at night if I left you here," Hawkins continued, "but what would I say to Claire?"

The rifle shook as Curran's strength began to fail

him. Hawkins calmly reached down and took the gun from his hand.

"You asshole," Curran gasped.

The sand around them began to kick up as gunfire pelted the beach. On the bluff, several Al Shuhada gunmen raced toward them. Hawkins reached down and grabbed Curran, carrying him into the water. Leary turned to fire back at the advancing gunmen. His rifle fired once, then quit—empty. He threw it down and followed Hawkins, Curran, and Ramos as they pushed their way out through the crashing surf.

The Al Shuhada fighters stopped at the water's edge, firing out at the SEALs. The choppy sea provided some protection as they bobbed out farther behind the swells.

Hawkins swam awkwardly, holding Curran's head above water as well as he could. Leary and Ramos were close together, swimming ahead.

The swell suddenly dropped, exposing them to the gunmen on the beach. Hawkins pinched Curran's nostrils closed and covered his mouth as they ducked under the water to escape the Arab gunfire. The swell rose again, protecting them as the SEALs bobbed back to the surface and began to swim again.

Ben Shaheed scanned the ocean as the swimmers escaped. He spied a nearby pier and a man crouched beside in his speedboat. Motioning for two of his men to follow him, he turned in the sand and ran down to the pier.

The startled boatman started to run. Shaheed shouted at him and fired a round into the sky. The terrified man stopped and put his hands on his head in surrender.

248

"Get back to your boat and start it," Shaheed barked in Arabic to the man.

The man stepped down into the speedboat and turned on the engine, while the three Al Shuhada men got in with him. Pointing his gun at the head of the hapless man, Shaheed ordered him out. The man jumped quickly up to the pier and watched as the armed men turned the boat out toward the open water, gunning the engine and throwing a plume of spray behind it.

Hawkins heard the approaching boat and treaded water as he looked around for the source of the noise. He'd just spotted the boat when he saw the back-blast of a rocket-propelled grenade.

"Oh, shit! RPG! Dive!" he shouted to the others, as he grabbed Curran and yanked him down, plunging far beneath the surface. The grenade exploded on the surface, sending shock waves through the water. Hawkins and Curran bobbed to the top almost immediately, blood flowing from their ears and noses.

The speedboat slowed. One of the gunmen pointed and yelled to Shaheed. He was pointing at Curran, floating on his back with his mouth open. Curran's face was covered with blood as he bobbed lifelessly in the water.

Shaheed directed the man at the wheel to bring the boat over to the body. As they pulled alongside the floating body, Shaheed took a boat hook from the side of the craft. Leaning over, he reached out with the hook and poked at the body. Curran's eyes snapped open, and his arm swung up from the water.

"Here," he said softly, as he lobbed a grenade into the boat.

One of the gunmen jumped forward in the boat, trying to retrieve the grenade. Shaheed jumped back and tripped, catching himself against the side. Hawkins's arm reached up over the gunwale and grabbed Shaheed by the back of the neck. Giving a quick jerk, Hawkins pulled the man out of the boat and into the water.

Leary swam up underneath Curran, pulling him away from the boat. Ramos surfaced and began to help Leary as they paddled frantically, putting distance between themselves and the boat.

The grenade exploded under the boat seats, causing the fuel to erupt in a black-tinged ball of orange flame. Pieces of fiberglass and Arab gunmen flew high into the air, then plummeted back to the ocean's surface.

Underneath the water, Shaheed struggled desperately to free himself from Hawkins's grip. He thrashed up to the surface briefly, only to be yanked down again.

The SEAL was in his element, and the Arab was not. Shaheed was aware of this. Reaching down to his ankle, he felt for his knife.

As they broke to the top of the water, Leary and Ramos watched as the Arab's arched arm shot up, a knife glistening in his hand. He plunged it down toward Hawkins. Another arm broke the surface and caught Shaheed's hand. The knife fell into the water.

As they struggled on the surface, Shaheed yelled out, "Help me! I can't swim!"

"Can't help you swim, you bastard," Hawkins sputtered. "But I'll help you DIE!"

Hawkins grabbed the terrorist by the neck and dove, dragging the man with him as he plunged deeper and deeper. Shaheed struggled in vain as Hawkins pulled him deeper into the water. Finally, Shaheed's body went limp, the last bubbles escaped from his mouth, and his eyes rolled back into his head.

Leary, Curran, and Ramos bobbed on the surface. The surface was covered with debris from the boat. They treaded water, waiting and watching for any sign of Hawkins. Leary began to shake his head and pointed to his watch.

Suddenly the water exploded in front of them as Hawkins hit the surface, loudly gasping for air. Ramos let out a whoop, and he and Leary paddled over to him. Curran floated motionlessly on his back, a thin smile on his lips, as he heard Hawkins gasp out loudly, "Yeah, boy, it's been a helluva day!"

About five hundred yards away from them, the black conning tower of the USS *Denver* broke the surface of the water.

Leary and Ramos pulled Curran up onto the deck of the submarine. Hawkins knelt down beside him. Curran blinked away the salt water in his eyes and held up his hand. Hawkins clasped it tightly.

"You brought us out," Curran gasped. "Nice going . . . boss."

"Hey, I just asked myself what would Curran do." Hawkins paused. "And then I improvised," he said, smiling.